BLINDSIDED

BLINDSIDED

by

Dick & Leigh Richmond—Donahue

Copyright © 1993 by Centric Foundation
First Reprint April 1994

CENTRIC FOUNDATION
P. O. Box 908
Maggie Valley, NC 28751
Phone (704) 627-9822

ISBN 0-943975-03-4

Published by
INTERDIMENSIONAL SCIENCES, INC.
P. O. Box 167
Lakemont, Georgia 30552

Manufactured in the United States

Front Cover
Idea and design by Dick & Leigh Richmond Donahue. GOR-
DON-MICHAEL SCALLION'S, FUTURE MAP OF THE UNITED
STATES, 1998-2001© reproduced with permission from Gordon-
Michael Scallion, Matrix Institute, RR1, Box 391, Westmoreland,
NH 03467

It's been a gaudy party. Kaleidoscopes of electrical and electronic rainbows; fantastic magics of computer; three cars to every
driver; rivers of oil; and the mad director shouting the old time
religions and handing out dope.

Now the clowns are disappearing, leaving the overflowing
ashtrays, the half-empty glasses, the spills, the bodies parked
twistedly in corners, the stench . . .

The bill is being presented—but who shall pay the charge? . .
. And in what coin? . . . And what's at stake? Why, nothing, except
the future of man . . .

Also by Leigh Richmond Donahue

Field Effect, the Pi Phase of Physics

Co–authored with the late Walt Richmond:

The Lost Millennium
The Probability Corner
Phase Two
Challenge the Hellmaker
Gallagher's Glacier
Shock Wave
Positive Charge

All the people in this story are fictitious; all the electronics are known and in use.

For Scott
. . . multi–talented Valkyrie of the mountains, who keeps an aura of sanity around her in a world going mad.

Contributing Editor: Tuc Stoodley

"The old order changeth yielding place to new, and God fulfills himself in many ways lest one good custom should corrupt the world . . ."

Alfred, Lord Tennyson
The Passing of Arthur

PRELUDE

The red light over the fireplace began to blink.

He stared at it, shocked for an instant into immobility.

Somebody had broken the signal light. Enemy or innocent?

It was only for an instant. Then he strode to the bedroom, belted on holster and pistol, reached the shotgun down from the high shelf. His face was grim.

He would wait five minutes. If there was no call from the house lower down the mountain, he'd sound the alarm, get down there fast and as quietly as possible.

He went to the deck and stared down the long cove. Mentally he checked where each of the others were.

His muscles tensed as the long minutes ticked by. He was, he realized, terrified. Sweating.

They had escaped the horror in New York. Barely. They had gotten to the mountains where they would be safe.

Where they would be safe?

He shuddered. How in the blue bloody blazing fires of hell could we have let it happen? It had been so abrupt. Or had it? When you could see the air you breathed?

One day we were civilized. The next, we weren't.

His stomach wrenched as the fourth minute passed . .

6

1

It was a comfortably messy room, its chairs overstuffed, its sectional couch strewn with pillows.

Books lined most of the walls to the ceiling. Paintings, warm with color, hung where there was space. The big windows in front looked over Central Park East.

Craig Gallagher sat in a large chair across from the TV watching the first football game of the season, his lanky form relaxed, his feet on a coffee table.

It was his favorite method for shutting out the world, for turning his mind from the insoluble problems presented by the news; by the plethora of magazines on every subject that he read; from the engineering problems that he saw everywhere, as well as in his own consulting work.

On the screen a quarterback was making an unsuccessful Hail Mary pass down the field as the clock in the corner went from 00:03 to 00:00.

His feet came to the floor with a thud, and he rose, stretching, his wide shoulders making a V of his tall body. He brushed back unruly graying brown hair from his forehead.

Out of the corner of his eye he caught movement and turned to find his wife, Alexandra, known as Lex, wrapped in a huge fluffy white towel, waiting impatiently for his attention.

Craig smiled almost guiltily. Lex didn't like sports on what she called "the ubiquitous bash tube." She would never understand the fascination, nor the reasons for it, of watching what she considered twenty-two jocks trying to kill themselves over a ball.

She had been getting ready for her lecture tonight. It would be a good audience, he felt. Her latest book, Electronic Anthropology, had made the best seller list in the New York Times, and the response was showing in ticket sales.

He was infinitely proud of her, not only for her tiny, slender figure, but for the off-beat perspective with which she viewed the human species; for the lack of any authoritarian attitudes; for the wide-eyed delight with which she saw the world in general, and its major occupants in particular. For her bubbling enthusiasms.

Her face was serious now. "The water pressure," she was saying in a voice tuned to carry over the sounds of players leaving the field, of sportscasters analyzing what had been happening.

"What?" He refocused his attention. Picking up the beeper he turned the sound down.

"What water pressure?" he asked.

"Our water pressure. The water pressure in the shower. It's just piddling out. I could hardly get wet in it."

He laughed, walked over and kissed her naked shoulder. "Wait about fifteen minutes," he said. "Half time has just started. Most of the people in New York are probably headed for the bathroom."

"What's that got to do with . . ." She stopped.

"There are eight million or so bathrooms in Manhattan alone," he told her severely. "If you start eight million toilets flushing at once, you get low pressure."

"Engineers." Her voice lost its irritation. He could see her visualizing the gigantic rivers of water it would take to supply that much outflow. A fantastic thought, even for himself. When you added in Brooklyn, Queens and the Bronx, the picture could boggle the mind.

"Some of them two or three times," he told her teasingly. "People watch football in gangs. Four or five to a set, probably."

"But how about those at the games? At least sixty thousand?"

He grinned. "The Port–A–Potties will be doing a land office business. Just wait till the next half starts. You'll have plenty of water then."

She made a face, then curled herself onto the couch with the ease of a cat, lit a cigarette.

He watched her for a minute, then headed for the kitchen to fix a drink.

When he turned on the faucet, there was the barest dribble of water. He stared at it. She was more than right, and it was not just the half–time rush.

Picking up a dishcloth he wiped out the sink, then settled the strainer so that it cut off the drain. He left the dribble flowing.

Well, this would be another adventure. Lex would take it in stride. She always did. She'd given herself almost as rough a life as he had had—learning welding at ten in his uncle's welding shop. Climbing the high steel by the time he was sixteen. Earning his way through Stanford as a foreman, summers, on high structures.

He'd been tested by a psychiatrist once, and told that he was the most practical person at his level of intelligence that the man had ever tested. "Normally at that level it all goes off in theory," the psychiatrist had said.

Well, it was a good thing he was practical, for Lex was not. Her research, her findings, were the breath of life to her, and she neither knew nor cared whether she had a dime in her pocket. If she had enough to eat, she was delighted. If not, she barely noticed.

She loved the good things in life, but scarcely heeded if they were not there. Her computer was the only asset she held on to.

When he went back to the living room, Lex looked up. "Craig," she said half-seriously, "how on earth can you supply this many people with water without Lake Ontario or something dammed up right north of us, waiting? You'd have to have the Mississippi and the Hudson together, flowing into tunnels and into pipes and into buildings, and . . ."

He looked at her, his angular face become mock-grave. "Actually," he said in a bantering tone, "it's not possible. There's not that much water in the world, to supply a megapolis that stretches from Boston to Washington, including New York, the Jerseys, and the hinterlands."

She giggled. "You look like a talk-show host, bedeviling the audience."

He switched the TV sound back on. Half-time was over, and the game had begun again. She headed for the bathroom.

An hour later, the tube finally silenced, the shouting hordes gone from the screen, she was back, dressed and ready for the evening.

"How do I look?" she asked.

"The compleat anthropologist," he told her. "Gorgeous but subdued. Not quite businesslike, but verging. I'll get dressed, while you fix us a drink, will you? There'll be water in the sink by now.

He headed for their bedroom, feeling his face. He'd shaved this morning. It would do. The big double bed looked inviting. Fifteen minutes to get the kinks out?

The westering sun was streaming gold through the curtained windows. There was time. They could eat on the way to the hall .

9

. . but she was ready. It wouldn't be fair. She'd be apt to get pre—lecture jitters.

He smiled. Fiftyish, and she looked to be in her late thirties. Slender, yes. Shapely, well in a ripened sort of way. Not pretty, but she'd earned her face and it showed. Becoming, perhaps.

Where had all the years gone since he and Lex had met at a Georgetown coffee shop? He a graduate assistant, she finishing her undergraduate work, debating taking a sabbatical year to roam the world before starting graduate work.

He could see it clearly in his mind; the crowded tables, the intense debates; the juke playing; the excitement.

What had it been like then? Craig smiled to himself. Smoky— but of cigarette smoke. In those days hashish was something that had been the undoing of China; cocaine and heroin were a scourge the Chinese were ridding themselves of by the simple expedient of decapitating importers, dealers and users alike.

But in America? That was one stupidity America would never bend to. It wasn't even a real temptation. He'd been offered a joint once, but had refused it in disgust. How naive we were.

He had entered the coffee shop and looked around, spotted her and liked her animation. He'd made his way unceremoniously to her table, hardly big enough for the extra chair he'd hooked over, but the clatter and clamor of the place made it natural to pull close to hear. He was too big for the chair, so he'd turned it around and straddled it.

Intent voices were arguing at every table.

Young, the students were, he'd decided from the heights of his assistantship. Young, and wet behind the ears, but earnest. He listened quietly, getting the feel of them, and of her.

Almost everybody in the place had read Rachel Carson's Silent Spring. Were the pesticides really that bad?

Lex had spoken up. "We'll find out," she'd said. "We'll find out and do whatever is necessary."

"But we're feeding the world, and we can't do that without pesticides." It was the youngster on his left.

"If they are bad, it is up to us to find new answers." Lex's voice was determined. "We're the new generation. Ours is the future, and we care. We care enough to find answers that work."

They hadn't found answers, Craig thought. Ethiopians were starving, walking the areas where an eight foot deep, wide river once flowed. The dust bowls in America had increased. Pesticides and poisons were polluting the waters of all the rivers and lakes of the world. The aquifers were salt–invaded. . .

No, they hadn't found answers.

The subject changed abruptly. Military advisors in Vietnam had been given permission to fire back if fired on. Would Vietnam become another "police action?" Somebody said that it was unfashionable to declare war any more, since that took an act of Congress, and no Congress in its right mind would vote war. They left it to presidents to declare "police actions."

"We'd never, ever again vote in anybody who would declare police actions hither and yon." It was Lex again. Determined.

"They already have in Korea." It was the first time Craig had spoken up.

"Oh," Lex told him lightly, "that's over. It was a mistake. Everybody knows that."

"Over, except for 55,000 of our men on the demarcation line. It's still a case of the Chinese saying `let's you and him fight.'"

Had he always been a doomsayer? he asked himself. She'd always been a fighter, an optimist.

She had looked at him squarely for the first time, his wide shoulders scrunched over the muscled arms as he leaned on the table. Her eyes were alight for battle. "We've outgrown police actions and idiocies like that. Our generation will . . ."

He had laughed at her, superior in his graduate wisdom. "We wrecked your Brave New World years ago," he said. "Back in 1946. It was done with the Top Secret label."

She caught her breath. "Just what do you mean by that?"

"When almost anybody in power—the President, a member of Congress, anybody in the Defense Department—can put any-thing he wants to under the Top Secret label—you get power politics and power government, and no New Generation will change that until you bring government back into the open again. It started with atomic formulas, to protect the oil companies. It's a disease. It spreads."

11

She didn't believe him. She argued angrily, and he kept laughing at her. Her color was high, her eyes sparkling as she argued, and he decided she was the most attractive dish he'd been with in a long time, in spite of what he decided were her sophormoic views.

Later he had walked her to her tiny apartment. She had argued angrily all the way, he answering in monosyllables, until the door had closed behind them, and he had reached out.

She had hesitated only a moment, and then came into his arms, her anger turning to the passion he had hoped to find. It had been an instant decision for him. She was what he wanted.

The next day he had moved in; the tiny apartment strewn with his things; the mess ignored on both sides.

That had been in early October, 1960.

Three weeks later the country was suddenly put on Red Alert. Russia had put The Bomb—The Bombs—in Cuba.

The civilian part of the nation was paralyzed. Schools closed. Civil Defense units, long the laughing stock of the country, brought out unwieldly plans and tried to put them in force. They were ignored as each individual and family tried hastily to find a safety net that did not exist.

The military went into action. Tanks rolled down the thruways towards Miami. Civilian traffic was ruled off the main roads. SAC planes flew constant patrols, loaded for bear.

He had thrown their heaviest clothes, boots, blankets and pillows, into his Chevy convertible, and went looking for her. He found her, finally, crossing the campus to a class they found later had been canceled.

"I'm getting you out of Washington," he told her. "We're getting married."

"What a romantic proposal," she said caustically, but she didn't waste time getting in. Then she had added softly, almost under her breath, "If that's a question, the answer is yes."

That was Lex. Happy, sure that the world itself was an adventure, and ready to go along with it wherever it took her. Light on her feet. Change of direction to her was a normal pastime, and he did mean pastime. She swept along as though with the wind.

He had laughed and patted her knee. "I've known I'd have to marry you since the first hour we met. You were so completely obnoxious."

It had seemed odd that he himself felt absurdly happy as well, when the end of their world was hanging by a thread.

"I've got to have the right to protect you," he told her solemnly. "This isn't the first time we've been right up against bomb-out, you know. Before this it's been the Top Secret of all Top Secrets. If we get past this one, it probably won't be the last."

She was astonished.

"There have been three that I know of," he had added. "The one at Suez came the closest. Those are only the ones I know of, though."

Her surprise didn't startle him. Most people didn't know how close they had come to what was known now as "nuclear winter . . ." or how often.

She had snuggled down into her seat. "Oh, well," she said. "We got past 'em." Then, seeing the expression on his face, she'd added, "You're going to have to do the worrying for the family. I'm just not capable in that direction."

They had been married in a quiet town in the Shenandoah Valley in a white clapboard church with a tall steeple, while Kennedy and Khrushchev were eyeball to eyeball. Then Khrushchev blinked, and they could go home.

Has it been that long, Craig asked himself, that we have lived from crisis to crisis?

But they seem to come faster now, one after another after another, with no time to adjust. The pace has stepped up until it is almost like the upward curve, after the long slow build-up of an exponential equation.

History, he told himself, is a process, not a series of events— and perhaps we are on an exponential curve, and the long slow build-up is reaching to the final sharp curve upwards that peaks, on the oscilloscope, and then reappears instantly at the same distance below the center.

He shook himself and finished dressing—dark suit, tie; he hated ties, but this was Lex's occasion. Then he headed for the living room where Lex had a bourbon and water waiting, ice standing by.

"Look okay?" he asked briefly. "I think I'll phone the water department. See what the trouble is. We've still plenty of time."

"Let me put ice in your drink."

He handed it to her absently, picking up the phone book. He found the number, then put his hip on the table, dialed. The line was busy. Of course, he told himself. Then he dialed all but the last two digits, waited about ten seconds, then dialed the last two. It was an old trick he hadn't used in a coon's age. This time he got through.

It was a tape. "Until this problem is cleared, please turn off any hot water heaters and air conditioners. This is to prevent a burn-out of your heating elements. We are working on the problem. Meantime, please conserve water."

When he turned away, there was a frown on his face. "They're not saying what the problem is, nor how long it will take, but I gather it's city-wide. They're advising that we turn off our hot water heater and—it's not on right now—our air conditioner."

"You think it's serious?"

His face had a far-away look. He answered almost as though he were talking to himself. "Oh, it probably is. They're not saying—but the drought—but the downpours we've been having should have taken care of that." Then he looked down at her. "Fix me a second bourbon will you? While I get things turned off. And make it soda this time, instead of water."

"Oh?"

"When water gets low, it's apt to concentrate any pollutants."

He made a face and went off on his errands. After cutting things off he went to the kitchen. The sink was nearly full. Then he headed for the bathroom and was scrubbing the tub when Lex came in.

"What the hell do you think you're doing?" She held the two glasses in her hands.

He grinned at her. "Taking precautions to preserve, my pretty," he said. "If eight million or so people are going to be out of water, I do not propose that you and I shall be among them. I'm going to fill the tub."

"But they said to conserve." She put his drink on the vanity.

14

"That's right. We're going to conserve. Right in the bathtub. I'll be with you in a second."

She closed her mouth firmly in what Craig had come to call her stubborn minute, because it always vanished as quickly as it came.

"It will run over while we're out," she said.

"There's an overflow drain. Had you noticed?" He stoppered the tub, leaving the trickle running.

"You don't supply a city without plenty of backup." She was still arguing. "While we're gone the—the reservoirs?—will refill. Then we'll be in a mess. We'll be—wasting. Oh Craig, is it really so drastic? I know about the farmers' problems. But New York? And one of the best condos in the city?"

He laughed, took a gulp of his drink, and patted her butt. "You leave the worrying to me," he said happily. "I do enough for two."

Later, as they made their way to the elevator, he hesitated, glanced at the door to the stairwell, then pushed the button. There is nothing about a water shortage, he told himself severely, to cause problems with elevators.

"Something?" she asked.

He smiled quickly. "No. Just . . . a momentary aberration. We're on the fourth floor.

She looked at the door to the stair well, then back at him, and shook her head. "Let's do our walking in the street," she said. "Eat somewhere nearby. We both need the exercise."

They made their way through the marble lobby, past the uniformed doorman, and out into the darkening night. Lex took a deep breath, then laughed. He looked. Central Park was just across the way, but there was a huge truck and honking vehicles of all kinds. It smelled of exhaust. A sheet of newspaper wrapped itself against her leg, then blew away.

She grabbed his arm, smuggled under his shoulder. "My mistake," she said. "Let's call a cab."

"You've been remembering New York the way it was," he told her.

"Before it drowned in automobiles," she admitted. "The way it was. I don't think I really like it any more. We come down into the streets and it feels—well, alien."

"We'll walk a bit." Craig's voice was quiet. .

They stayed silent past the Plaza, past the spires of St. Patrick's, pushing through the crowds of Fifth Avenue. A panhandler tried to bar their way, but Craig pulled her past. She shuddered.

He looked down at her. "You're looking in the wrong direction," he said, his tone light. "You're looking at the detritous. At the cup half—empty. Look up. It's half– full."

She held his arm tightly, letting her eyes follow the lines of Rockefeller Center up and up—letting herself see the outlines of the city as it reached across the sky.

But Craig caught his breath. For a minute the huge buildings seemed to tower over them, ready to fall, to crush . . . each filled with humans, each human without water? Thirsty. A desert of people, high in the unforgiving buildings . . .

The moment passed, and the tall buildings against the darkening sky cast their spell. Lights. A glory of lights. And the buildings themselves seemed to be lifting, lifting . . .

"New York was never beautiful below," he said. "Not for fifty years. It's grimy, and it's drowning in automobiles. But the stars are in the buildings. Look at them. Thousands and thousands of jewels, spread out for your admiration."

And, yes, they are beautiful, he thought. The half–full part of New York. And the people are like unto them. The upstairs people where the lights are; the downstairs people who have lights but are verging; and the street people, who range from the alive through the undercultured to the abandoned. Half–empty. And all in one tremendous over–populated cage together.

They hurry along, he thought, lost in their own lives, each in his own world, fighting his own battles. Doing their loving and being loved . . . except for those who rot huddled over ventilators from the buildings. What made them drop out of mainstream America? Are we that great a nation to let such happen?

Abruptly he felt uneasy again. Frightened. You have lived here for years, he scolded himself. Why, suddenly, should you become wary?

Yet the city seemed unfamiliar, to have assumed a new perspective; to loom over them, a monster, gloating as though in warning.

Suddenly he laughed aloud—at himself, at gloom in general, at the whole discombobulated world.

He reached down and swung her off her feet in a circle that scattered nearby pedestrians.

"I," he said, "am taking you to the Twenty-One for a gala dinner before I let you go on stage to teach people what they're all about."

When they arrived, Lex was radiant, her eyes sparkling, her gaiety contagious. They were greeted by name by the maitre d' and shown past a waiting line to a corner table.

They ordered martinis, and Lex gazed cheerfully around at the cocktail hour crowd. She put an affectionate hand on his arm. "You have the loveliest ideas," she said.

As the drinks were served a pudgy, slightly balding man came trotting over. He had the face of a Pekingese and, Craig decided, seemed to be wagging an invisible tail.

"Lex Gallagher!" he exclaimed. "I'm Bill Simon of the Post. What a treat! I see I got here at the right time. Your book set my teeth on edge!

"So we're evolutionary, are we? You'd hardly know it to look at the mess we've gotten ourselves into!"

He kept prattling on, his voice adding exclamation marks to every sentence. Craig began to wonder how he got the material for the column Lex read almost daily. He didn't wait for answers, nor make room for her in his chatter.

But then, Craig realized, he didn't need quotes. It was a gossip column, and the way it would run would be—he could almost quote it verbatim as it would appear in tomorrow's paper:

"At the Twenty-One I ran into Lex Gallagher, that delightful and quite stunningly dressed anthropologist who talks in multi-syllabic terms of what most of us never even dreamed, but who is so chic you'd hardly notice. You really must read her <u>Electronic Anthropology</u>, though you may find her a little far out . . ."

INTERLUDE

The Earth felt glutted, abused.

The units of the scurrying life form on her crust had doubled by the decade over the past six thousand years until they had become swarms.

At first they had been quiescent; had made themselves a part of her, hardly noticeable as they pushed across her surfaces on foot and then on horseback, nourishing her soil, greening her plantings; occasionally bothersome, but in a slow, almost gentle manner.

It was different now. Now the swarms nested everywhere. Now they had harnessed the lightning and shot electronic arrows through her bowels and through her atmosphere, altering the magnetic melts within her; changing the stately manner of her seasons. They dug out her metals and ripped at her surface with metallic claws. They sprinkled obscene matter across her skin, buried arsenals of hate, fouled her waters, transformed even the electromagnetic envelope which held her and kept her in the constancy of rotation that had been her comfort.

They were in their billions now; and reproducing on an exponential scale . . . Man, the only animal that dirties his own nest . . .

2

At the small auditorium underneath Lincoln Center, Lex was greeted by her hostess of the evening, and Craig made his way to the back where he could watch the audience as well as his wife. He picked an aisle seat where his legs could get extra room.

The group of around eighty was in good part male, which pleased him. She had a widespread reputation. Now that her latest book was proclaimed a best seller, it was growing rapidly.

He watched her tiny figure at the podium, assured, he decided, in spite of the butterflies he knew to be in her stomach. She always had butterflies before a lecture, but they disappeared rapidly. Her voice reached him clearly.

"Most people think of anthropology," she was saying, "as exemplified in one of its branches—social anthropology, the study of various tribes as they approach civilization. Or archaeo-logical anthropology, the study of ancient peoples as they began to discover tools.

"But anthropology is confined to neither of these. It is the study of the human being. The gestalt human, as he exists today, did then, and will exist in the future.

"All studies of the human are part of anthropology, even psychiatry, though you needn't tell your pet shrink that . . . ."

She got the expected laugh, and Craig realized with a start that a good many of these people probably did have pet shrinks; were trying desperately to find their way out of the tensions you could feel . . . not just here in New York, but all over the world, wherever you went. A civilization shaking itself to pieces with tensions . . .

"You probably think of evolution as something that happened in the distant past," she was saying. "Yet one of the largest and most abrupt evolutionary steps was taken by the human within the past seventy years, and it is hardly recognized for what it is."

She paused, took a sip of water, looked over her audience to be sure they had absorbed her last statement.

My completely original wife, Craig thought. Nobody had looked at her premises until she had written her recent books, and now it was as though what she had to say had been known forever.

There was nothing commanding about her; nothing to make anyone conscious of the years of work, the years of refusing to accept normal patterns, that had gone into the results she had found; and had verified.

She looked so tiny behind that podium; so pert, and—well, young for all her years.

Anthropologist? She'd broken the mold on that one. Anthropologists were supposed to go into the depths of Africa to study tribes who still clung to ancient habits and beliefs.

Lex had gone into the highways and byways of the world around her, to study what the human was like today—not as a psychiatrist, not watching their foibles; but to study the whole human; the good, the bad, the indifferent.

She had gotten herself into a mob of gangsters during one summer vacation from college; she had gotten a job working in one of the wealthiest homes in the nation, another. And for one vacation, she had lived with the homeless as one of themselves. On the streets. Without money in her pocket. Quite often, without eating.

"The high, the desperate and the depraved," she had explained to him once. "I want to know what homo sapiens is today. And that you don't find out in the textbooks."

He was glad that had been in the old days, before drugs had taken over the streets.

She had started college determined to become a neuro- psychiatrist, taking pre-med and psychology courses. "But their terms weren't broad enough," she explained. "Not even the medical parts. The medics were looking at bodies; and the psychiatrists were looking at neuroses; and never the twain could see what was walking the streets around them."

She'd taken classes in biochemistry, and in the structure of the mind and body . . . "But the answers weren't there," she admitted.

She'd specialized in ancient history, trying to find the patterns behind what the textbooks had to say; and in more modern history, the patterns of movement of mankind across the face of his planet.

"It has all been fascinating," she told him once. "I have some answers; but they're so far out I can't get anyone to listen."

She had never thought of herself as an "authority." Not on any subject. She had found some answers, and she had written a couple of books, and she still looked at the human as the most exciting subject that existed. Not his past—his present. His potential.

"The evolution of man starts back in infinity; you can watch it to here. But it doesn't stop here, unless we stop it. It could go on and on and on. The potential is there."

Tiny. Delightful. Passionate. And, to his way of thinking, beautiful.

He felt both proud and protective—and he tried to keep the protective from baracading her from the world she had explored so recklessly before.

Now that their children were grown and gone, he knew that she might suddenly decide to go out into the highways and byways again, unencumbered—and that he must let her.

It would frighten and dismay him, for she was so vulnerable in her thirst for knowledge. She would come back, but he would be frightened.

They were listening now. Intently and with the deepest respect.

"Mankind evolved," she was saying, "subject to a 7.83 cycles per second pulse. That is the electronic pulse–rate of Planet Earth. It is a constant pulsing, very like the constant heartbeat in your own body.

"Man evolved in tune with that pulsing, from the beginning. The heartbeat of his mother—Mother Earth—and humankind in her womb."

He settled back, trying to make himself more comfortable.

It was a new thought to most of them, and she gave it a moment to sink in. Then, with a quick smile, she went on.

"It was not until this century that man developed his own pulsing electrical currents that began to blot out the pulse-beat in which he had been nurtured.

"You have heard it said that more progress has been made in the last seventy years than in all of history combined. And that is true. But did you look—did you ask—what was the factor that initiated that dramatic change? What made it possible—what made it inevitable?"

She paused again.

"This nation was wired, comparatively over night, for sixty cycle per second alternating current.

21

"An alternating cycle current broadcasts—and it is a nerve stimulus of the first order. Your entire nervous system, including your brain, is like an antenna, receiving that broadcast and reacting to it. Speeding up. Becoming more effective."

She paused again.

"You may think of electricity as within the wires in the walls of your home; or within the wires of the power lines that web this nation.

"It's carried by those wires, yes. But the magnetic field it creates reaches far beyond those wires, and it pulses in your body, day and night, invisible and unrecognized, almost wherever you are. From birth until death you `dance' now to that sixty cycle pulse.

"The sixty cycle broadcast had the effect of increasing the intelligence of the nation."

She took a sip of water, allowing the idea to sink in. Then she continued. "It was in the late 1800s that electricity was first introduced, first as a direct current which had little effect, then as an alternating current. Almost by happenstance—not because it was beneficent, although it is, but because the first generator was set at that frequency, the sixty cycles were chosen in this country. Europe chose fifty cycles—less effective on the brain.

She looked over her audience slowly. "There were scattered effects from the first installations—before the '20s.

"But have you noticed what happened when this whole nation became wired, and the stimulus hit almost everybody? A tremendous intoxication of the brain and nervous system.

"Almost overnight our brains came alive. We went from the horse—ten miles an hour—to the car, to the plane. From the horse-drawn plow to the tractor. From communication by ship to communication by satellite. From the very slow lane—walking or horseback—to the very fast lane. In little over seven decades.

"It has been a very short maturity . . ."

Craig, listening, felt suspended between two worlds—the solid reality of the auditorium and the people around him; and the electrical forces, invisible to his five senses, but no less real, that coursed constantly through his system, tossing him, a chip on an unseen ocean . . . .

The lecture was over at the appointed hour, but the questions and answers were becoming interminable. Finally their hostess rose and reminded the group that this was only the first of Mrs. Gallagher's three lectures, that the hour was late. She could autograph their books tomorrow.

They were making their way towards the ranks of taxis outside when a burly young man in sweat shirt and jeans grabbed Lex's arm, swinging her to face him, glowering in her face.

Craig reached to shove him off, then realized it was the lecture he was talking about.

"You preach a good sermon," he was saying, "but you're practically pre-historic."

Craig hesitated, astonished, his hand on the young man's shoulder. Most people considered Lex too far out for comfort. Had this one been in the audience? He didn't look as though he could afford the fee, but . . . .

"You _are_ ahead of most idiots." The voice was gruff, angry. "But . . . there's a whole new spectra of electronics out there that you didn't even mention. Probably don't even know about, at that, because it was first used as a weapon. But it sure affects your precious gestalt human."

She was listening.

"It's the electronics of _time_!" His voice was explosive. "It's a whole new area, radically different.

"You're used to the electro/magnetic system, the EM cycles, that give you electricity, TV, radar, computers—the works. They all broadcast, and they all affect you. That's _space_ electronics.

"The new spectra are the dialectro/diamagnetic cycles. DEM for short. They're different. They're in _time_. They're opposed to space. They go through the earth as though it weren't there, because they're not spatial. They affect you. They affect the _time_ half of you.

"You're right that the introduction of electricity brought our _spatial_ brains awake. Our EM brain. It hurt, like any birthing hurts. You wouldn't remember. It hurt like mad, but it worked. All kinds of ruckus, but we woke up. Half our brains got born, so to speak. And those who didn't wake up were left in the dust."

"Both halves of our brains came alive."

"Yeah. Both halves of our spatial brains. But you've got the other half of you and its brain. The time half. The DEM half. What you call the soul or the spirit or the psyche, or the aura. The opposed half. That's what I mean."

"You're talking religion. Or spiritualism. Or both."

"I am not. I'm talking electronics. The time spectra were discovered around thirty years ago, and they're just being really developed. We've been broadcasting in them—using them as a weapon—for the past ten or so years.

"Your body is in the EM—the space spectra. So are electricity and TV and radar. Your other half is in the DEM—the time spectra. So are the DEM broadcasts, and they hit your emotions with a bang.

"Those broadcasts can be good, bad or indifferent—tune 'em the way you want. They make one of the best weapons in the business. They can be white magic or black magic or voodoo. But they're bringing the time half of your brain awake. Just like that sixty cycle EM alternating current brought the space half of your brain awake."

She looked at him impatiently. "Why don't we know we've got a time half?" she asked.

"Oh, some of the adepts suspect it . . . religious, spiritualists, voodooists. But, hell, your whole precious gestalt human—the whole being—is an alternating frequency system. We've just discovered the electronics of the `other half.' Using it for over ten years, and just finding out what it is.

"You, the earth, everything is on an alternating frequency system. Blinks on and off. EM/DEM. Space/time. Just like an electric light blinks on and off.

"You don't see it, you can't touch it, because the EM half, the spatial half, is `off' when the time half is `on.' And because the brain in the time half is still incubating. Just coming awake.

"You've been living in an EM spectra blizzard—sixty cycles, high frequency TV, radar. They brought that half of your brain awake.

"Now we're broadcasting in the DEM—the time spectra. And it's bringing the DEM half of your brain awake.

"Then," he said, "you'll be a whole person. Except for those who can't handle it, and they'll just fade out."

He shoved his hands in his pockets angrily, and started to turn away, but she put her hand on his arm to restrain him.

"Tell me more," she said insistently.

"Tell you? You can see it all around. You gotta look." He pulled his arm away.

"I'd like to talk to you," she said. "Who are you?"

"Name's Uriah Malchek. Yuri."

"When can I see you?"

He grinned, an impish grin that turned his face from grim to sardonic. Why, he resembles a satyr, Craig thought. A lean face, accenting high cheek bones and a long beak of a nose. The figure almost squat but powerful.

The jeans and sweat shirt might be inappropriate to the occasion, but they were fresh, clean. His face was smooth–shaven; his dark hair tousled, unruly, falling to his shoulders but trimmed. His aerobic sneakers looked to be L. L. Bean. His hands large, expressive, the nails clean.

So young—late twenties?—so intense. As we used to be intense, Craig thought.

"I live way the hell and gone in Pennsylvania," he said. "I read your book and drove in to listen. It's only a couple of hours."

Lex smiled. "If we may, we'll drive way the hell and gone up into Pennsylvania. You came to listen to me. I'd like to listen to you."

Yuri pulled a small note book from his pocket, a pen lodged in the neck of his sweat shirt, and began to write. Then he turned to Craig.

"This is my name and phone number," he said. "And this is how you find me." He was sketching rapidly. "You turn off the Interstate, here, take a right . . ."

Craig listened carefully and took the paper, slipped it into his pocket.

"It will be couple of weeks," Lex was saying. "We'll phone."

Back at the condo, he fixed drinks while she put on her pajamas and dressing gown, exhausted but shining.

"That young man—Yuri?—" she said. "So young. so angry. I didn't follow what he was talking about. But—I have a need to know. We'll go find him. Soon." Then, "It went well?"

"You know darned well it went well. Terrific." He kissed her and handed her a bourbon and soda.

"Soda?" she asked. "No ice" Then she remembered. "No water?"

"I should have gotten bottled water on the way back. For drinking and ice cubes."

"There's still a trickle to shower in," she suggested. "You didn't shower before we left."

"Not now," he said. "And . . . don't flush the toilet unless . . ."

She giggled. "Primitive living in the finest Manhattan condos. Shall I see if we have flint and steel to start a fire?" She pulled out a cigarette and leaned forward to the table lighter.

"There's your flint and steel," he told her. "That's what a lighter is, flint and steel and a gas product, handily packaged."

She looked at it in surprise. "I never thought of that. We <u>are</u> Boy Scouts. Prepared." Then, "Oh, Craig, how long will this go on?"

"It may take a while to get this one fixed. The system's pretty old. There are going to be breakdowns in lots of systems, I'd think; until somebody gets really serious about fixing them. It will cost billions to get a good substructure going'; but we built the old one. We ought to be able to rebuild to suit."

"You're really taking our trickling water seriously, aren't you?"

He walked to the window, looked out at the lights in the buildings across the park. Then, hands in his pockets he leaned against the drapes, his rangy figure carrying out the dark stripes of the material.

"I am," he said. "Indeed I am. Breakdowns and fix ups will probably be sporadic at first. But cumulative I'd think we're looking at the sins of the fathers being visited on the children . . . and it just might be unto the third and fourth generation, because we're not taking the time—and money—to repair what we built."

Lex laughed. "We've got a lot of repair work to do. Our water, when it runs, is full of pesticides and junk—and chlorine to clean it up. And acid rain getting into it. Acid rain doesn't just kill trees—it falls on the land and into the water. And there's the smog . . . ."

"Never mind," he said. "The ecologists are after the big bears. Let's leave it to them. But meantime, it's going to get right uncomfortable here until they fix this break. Why don't we take a vacation? Get the car and take a trip?"

"Oh, they'll have it fixed by tomorrow."

"Yeah. Then stutter and start, stutter and stop. Might take two weeks. And us living in a mess."

"They ought to call you in as consulting engineer. You're so bull–dogged stubborn you'd frown at it and it would fix itself."

He smiled. "I think that was a compliment. Maybe."

"Anyhow, I've got two more lectures, tomorrow and the next day. I wish I knew what that youngster, Yuri, was talking about. That other half . . ."

"That first half of you can get right . . . I started to say `dirty,' but I meant unwashed. Oh, well. We've got a sink and a half–tubful of water. We can last two more days."

"Then there's the publisher's party in two weeks."

"Hell's fire. We could be back in two weeks. Make you fresh for the party. And by then the water should be flowing full. We could even stop to see your young satyr."

"Satyr?"

"Yuri. He looks like one when he grins."

She nodded happily. "That would be fun. I was planning to start my next book right after the lectures, but . . ."

"Take your lap–top along. We'll go see Jeff and Terry too, and inhale the fresh air of the mountains. You could write about all the disasters looming . . . and why we should do drastic things about them immediately, if not sooner."

"You are the consulting engineer of the family. You're the one who has to tend to Impending Disasters, like all repair work we've put off for too long; and the state of the ecology. I'll content myself with good old homo sapiens himself, and whether he has two brains or one. Fascinating idea," she added.

"You could call the next book `You and You.'"

She giggled. "Or `Two and Two'! If the one brain has two halves, the other should have two as well."

"Two and two are four. Call the book `Are We Each a Crowd?'"

They were both laughing as he picked her up and carried her in to the bed. They were still laughing as he pulled her pajamas off and began stroking her body.

"First time I ever made love to a crowd," he said.

She sighed happily. "My crowd will take on your crowd any day of the week. And may the best crowd win." Then forgot the whole subject as their bodies locked together and passion rose to engulf them.

INTERLUDE

Russia was the first to explore the potential of the time frequencies—the DEM structure of the hitherto unrecognized "other half" of the universe.

Powerful forces lay there. They could be used as a weapon.

It was in 1959 that Khrushchev first intimated the existence of the new weapon.

He came to the United Nations and announced that they had better make peace immediately; that Russia had a weapon more effective than The Bomb, and would use it.

The nations of the U.N. failed to come to heel, and in frustration the Russian Premier pounded the table with his shoe; an act that only served to make him a laughing stock.

Khrushchev's passionate threat was premature. It took years to develop the techniques to real effectiveness. Early unnoticed experiments were made on small groups, conferences mostly, held in nearby countries where they could be monitored.

The results were to Russia's liking. The groups showed violent symptoms of headaches, nausea, disorientation, and best of all the new broadcasts hit the emotions, producing fear, grief and guilt.

The first bombardment to be recognized for what it was was used against the American Embassy in Moscow. The reaction was immediate, the protests adamant.

It became known—by those who knew—as the Woodpecker Syndrome, the name taken from the dotting sound that impinged on normal electronic reception.

As her expertise grew, Russia began bombarding the peoples of the U.S.A. with the same frequencies; with the same results. That was not difficult, since the time spectra frequencies went through the spatial earth as though it were not there. That those broadcasts affected the planet's "other half" was not recognized.

It did not take long for the experts in the U.S.A. to find the new spectra, nor to begin bombarding the peoples of Russia.

China was the third in line, but kept her own broadcasts focused on her own people. They were recalcitrant, hard to control in their great numbers. She would control them.

That there were beneficent uses for these spectra all three nations knew. They were disregarded.

The peoples of all three nations, as well as others nearby, responded with growing restlessness. The first violent physical symptoms ameliorated. Their emotional reactions rose from fear, grief and guilt to hate, to covert anger, to overt anger.

The bombardments on all three fronts increased. The anger of the peoples increased.

China was the first to notice the new results. Instead of groveling, her people were becoming angry, and their anger focused against their own impotence.

It wasn't an overall result. Individuals reacted to the powerful stimulus each in his own way. The young were the first to reach anger and rebel. They began to gather in Tiananmen Square and other places.

Within days the cause became obvious to the Chinese experts of Tao with their ancient memories of such.

The Chinese broadcasts were shut off, and those in power began turning the angers of their people outward towards their neighbors.

Russia and the United States were slower to notice. It was not until The Wall was torn down, almost overnight; until revolutions sprung to life all over the U.S.S.R.; until in the U.S. crime and drugs became overwhelming, that the two nations, by mutual consent, shut off the broadcasts.

They were already too late.

3

Craig slipped out of bed next morning and dressed quietly. He scribbled a note to Lex, left it in the bathroom where the water was still a trickle, three-quarters full now. She would sleep late after the lecture.

He'd get coffee out somewhere. It was Saturday, but he would go to the office, square away the stuff he was working on so he could leave for a bit.

It was a brilliant, clear day with the first tang of crispness in the air to indicate that summer was nearly over.

The city's tremendous vitality took hold of him, as it usually did. New York was an exciting place—to look at, to walk in, to experience. What a helluva city, he thought. All vertical lines and fast motion. Intense. He felt great. Sure, it had its faults. Sure, its underpinnings were getting shabbier than could be believed. But we built it; we can fix it.

He walked over to Park Avenue and turned to his right, his long stride, unhampered by Lex's shorter steps, taking him at a fast pace.

Already the streets and sidewalks were full.

As he reached Grand Central Station a slender figure pushed through the heavy doors and turned down the street ahead of him. Her hair was soft and straight, and fell to her shoulders, which pleased him. The fuzzy hair-dos of today were not to his liking. She wore a full gray shirt which swirled about her long legs, and a tiny gray jacket that just missed the top of the skirt. Her heels were high, but not spiked, and she walked with a swing that gave her hips a sinuous movement he found delightful.

Swishy young broad, he thought. Wonder if that swish would carry over to bed? He laughed, remembering a magazine article that said a man doesn't think of sex oftener than every twenty seconds. You old fool, he scolded himself, you have all you can handle at home.

But she was a pleasure to watch; a slender young thing, eager, full of vitality, of curiosity, making her way down the streets of America's greatest city, ready to create her own niche in a society that held, in her mind, the promise that youth and energy could give it. Making her way into a future.

Suddenly his eyes unfocused, and he was looking at the decrepit support structure that made the life she lived possible. The trains—Westchester, at a guess from the cut of her clothes. The streets that were paved over the vast complex of wires and pipes and subways that underlay the city. The elevator that would take her to the floor where she worked. The electricity that powered the city. The trucks, the constant trucks, that supplied the needed goods. The money and credit cards, those vast and complicated exchanges that kept track of the economic flows that were modern man's barter system. The shops and restaurants; the intermingling of people and things; the music and laughter. And the sadness.

How had man, in a haphazard and almost thoughtless way, created a structure so much more complicated than an automobile, or even a computer—bit by growing bit, from the farms of the Dutch to the gigantic towers of the millions . . .until you had the intricate interrelationships between city and people, between static mechanisms and the volatile, changing, demanding dynamics of movement and purpose, each with his own, each to his own goal?

I'm doing the standing-in-awe department, he thought, as he watched the girl turn towards Madison and Fifth.

The structure . . . the interwoven structure of streets and wires and traffic lights and telephones and computers and vehicles and building—the structure supports the people, and the people are an intricate part of the structure, no one of them possible of controlling the whole; no one of them possible of independence of the whole.

Such a magnificent support structure—and all to make it possible for a young girl to trip becomingly down the street in search, whether she knew it or not, of a future of love and happiness and dancing and dreaming, and children of her own.

Was he witnessing the first symptoms of the crumbling of the structure? It's only water that I see. A temporary symptom. But a major part of the support system, and the interrelationships are there.

And . . . when an interdependent system shows symptoms of collapse, what factors are next? Disease. How do you operate a hospital without water? But more. When you stir an ant hill, panic starts. Riots? Probably. Senseless. Each person fighting for his own survival, against his own fears. Runs on banks, just because.

If the electricity went too—as it could, he realized; it quite possibly could—no trains, no subway, no elevators. No gasoline.

He saw the young girl in his mind again. Scared. Running. Not knowing where to go. Panicked. Probably victimized—and no way off the island that had become a prison. The heel of one shoe was broken. Her skirt was bedraggled; her purse gone; her hair— he didn't even want to <u>think</u> about her hair . . .

The vision vanished as quickly as it had come. He looked again at the tall buildings. They looked suddenly forbidding.

It's time to run, he thought. Now. Before—before what?

He shook himself. What in the blue bloody blazing nether regions of hell did he think he was doing? One dripping faucet, and he was concocting scenes of the very living end.

The city and its teeming life felt solid, secure again. Yet the instinct was there.

He reached the building that held his office, looked up at its vertical structure and found himself hesitating. Damnation, he thought. This is getting ridiculous. Then: Do other people feel insecure in a city these days, or is it just the engineer in me, looking for more cracks where I've seen one? But he turned away, without going up.

Instead, he took a taxi to Abercrombie Fitch and made his way to the upper story belt department, where he found two money belts. The economic system, he was thinking as he brought out his credit card, is as complex as is the structure of the city itself. The card was instantly registered on the computer console, verified, and somewhere—out there—somewhere in a distant terminal, in another slightly less complex city, his account was debited for the amount.

What a magnificent organism is our economy, he thought.

Next, to the bank. He'd need money for their trip; and on the road a good part of it should go in the two belts. The rest?

He asked for one thousand, half in hundreds, the other in twenties. The hundreds would fit in the belts; the rest in his wallet. In a crunch, he heard himself thinking, when survival is at stake, common commerce—the commerce of the streets and shops— the gas stations—changes. "Do you want the gas or don't you?" he could hear a gruff voice saying as he held out a hundred dollar bill for a five dollar purchase, and asked for change.

Survival! He was thinking in terms of survival! And all that had happened was a dripping faucet . . . .

He'd met survivalists before and laughed at them. Smug. Secure, he'd been. He laughed at himself; but he didn't change his specifications.

He watched the teller as she entered the sum and his account number into her computer terminal. But suppose, he rationalized his feelings, computer worms and viruses should reach the terminals. They were a growing hazard.

He looked around at the solid bank structure, at the coiffed teller, at the movement of people. We are simply taking a vacation during a very temporary but uncomfortable situation, he admonished himself. You do not need to go off the deep end.

On the way home, he stopped at store after store, trying to buy bottled water. Sold out, wherever he went. Of course, he thought. He bought the last of the soda in three different groceries, keeping his taxi waiting. There were none of the colas left, anywhere, as far as he could discover.

I'm a bit late, he told himself. Should have thought of this last night.

At the apartment he put his packages on the kitchen table. He found Lex in the den on the exercycle, dressed in a blue sweat suit, her long hair swept back into a bun, her face glistening with perspiration. She stopped the cycle when she saw him, waited for his kiss, then began pumping the cycle slowly.

"I thought you'd sleep all day, the way you were pounding your ear at five o'clock. Then I woke and your weren't there."

"I was awake most of the night."

He pulled the chair from his side of their big double desk and sat down facing her.

"I know you were awake most of the night," she told him. "I saw the ash trays full. I must have slept like a log. I wasn't even conscious that you weren't beside me. Or that you left early. Did you fix things at the office so we can take off?"

"Changed my mind. Decided to phone instead. You always sleep heavily after a lecture," he added. Then: "I have a suggestion."

"Okay." She got off the cycle, pulled a tissue from a nearby box and wiped her forehead. Then she hooked her hip over the seat of the cycle and waited.

"Why don't I get the car and we pack it? Be ready to leave right after your lecture Sunday night? We have to be back for your publisher's party in two weeks. That would give us an extra day."

She nodded. "Makes sense. I'm really looking forward to the trip! We've been sticking around home base too long." She stretched. "It'll be fun being out in the great open spaces. I like being part of the millions when everything is going right. But it gets a bit grim when you have to think twice before reaching for a drink . . . and then it's soda not water."

He smiled. "I like being part of the millions, too, when things go right. Being among those who are recognized and count in the accounting. But not right now. I've got itchy feet."

"You just don't like being subject to problems somebody else is solving for you. Now, if they'd call you in to help, I wouldn't be able to get you out of here with a crowbar. Do you suppose Kathy and Brian could take time off and go for a vacation with us? We could meet them at Jeff and Terry's and have a family get-together. Ride their horses; grill steaks in the outdoors . . ."

"Kathy would love it. She's like you—take off in a minute, no matter what was up. But our son-in-law? Brian? Maybe, I'll phone."

When he reached their daughter in Tampa, she sounded happy. Their perennial optimist, he thought. Like her mother. She was their number two child, pert and blond and always busy. "Busy Bee" they'd called her. She and Brian were planning to wait before having babies. "Makes it easier in this economy," she'd told him.

He talked inanities for a minute, to get the feel of her, before asking, "How's your water supply? Ours is temporarily discom-bobulated, and we're going to take a vacation."

"Oh, we've been on water hours for a week." Her voice was lilting, undismayed. "I understand that Fort Lauderdale and Miami just went on them, too. Outside the city, they've got helicopters out, watching for wasters. One landscaper was fined heavily for watering plants that weren't for food. And they've got squads of policemen watching . . . ."

"What," he asked, "are water hours?"

"You don't <u>know</u>? Lucky you. The city turns the water on in each section for about two hours a day. Most of the corporations have arranged their schedules so people can get home for their hours. What people do who live too far from their jobs to get home, I don't know. Maybe neighbors? It's a mess."

She paused for a minute, and he held the phone thoughtfully. Then: "We're going to Jeff and Terry's for a couple of weeks, until this is over. Why don't you two join us? Make it a family reunion? Let people solve things, then come back?"

She laughed happily. "Oh, it's a mess, but we'll survive. People do, you know. Brian's in the middle of a big engineering job for Weston, and I've got six stores to inventory. It sounds like fun, but we'll take a rain-check. Give them our love."

When he rang off, he turned to Lex. "It's not just here," he said, and told her about water hours in South Florida.

There was a frown on his face as he dialed their son. Jeff, tall, rather gangling; with dark hair that fell over his forehead. He supported a wife, two children and four horses by writing mystery books; turning them out, Craig felt, like a short-order cook. The books were popular, which was fortunate in his father's view, because horses were expensive, even when you had lots of mountain with medium pasture.

Craig and Lex had teased Jeff by asking whether, in a pinch, he'd choose the horses or the children, and had decided long since that all horse people were crazy.

When Jeff answered, Craig wasted no words. "How's your water supply?" he asked. If Jeff was startled by the abruptness of the question, he didn't sound it.

"Our spring dried up last summer," he answered. "We ported water from the creek for a bit, then found another spring up the mountain. It's not on our land, but we hooked in without asking. We had some rain this summer and we're all right for now. If we have another drought, we'll have to drill a well, though last summer wells dried up too.

"You heard about the hay lift last summer?" he went on. "The dairy men were having to slaughter cows because they hadn't been able to make a crop. The Midwest trucked hay in for free. This year we've had some rain, and we've been returning the hay to the Plains States. The rain belt was from lower Texas, up through this area, to New England. Not too much, but the crops came in. The Plains were dry."

"If we came up for a few days, would you have enough for us too?"

"Hey! Wonderful! And yes."

"See you in a few days, then."

Lex had been in the bedroom packing and hadn't listened to the second call. Now he poked his head in there.

"Get the car," she said. "I'm almost packed. Then I want to walk Fifth Avenue. Goggle at the stores. Maybe buy something, though I don't need a darn thing. You're such a good provider, Luv."

He made one more phone call, to the garage, before he left. When he got there, they were just bringing his red Tercel down the lift. He stood watching the system, straddle–legged, his whip-cord body still, eyes intent.

Elevator, he thought. What goes next? When the stress points of a structure begin to show cracks, you look for the points where the cracks will put pressure. You watch for the next break as one break puts more load on the next factor. That's just good engineering.

Water is a major stress factor. Next unto it is power. Electricity. You're an idiot, he told himself, but he got into the car and circled back to the east. On Lexington he found a ramp–garage. He stopped and finally found the tiny cubicle–office.

Inside was a big–bellied hulk of a man, two days' stubble on his cheeks, the stub of a cigar clenched in his teeth.

"Cost ya," the man said.

Space rentals were listed on a dirty card on the wall. Craig looked at them.

"Full up." The cigar stub was clamped until it pointed up.

Craig pulled out a ten spot. The man looked at it and spat. Craig made his gesture tentative as he added a twenty. The man nodded. "One space," he said shortly. Fourth ramp up. Number 431."

The thirty disappeared. Craig pulled out the rental fee, de-manded a receipt, finally got it. Smothering his annoyance he drove off. Maybe the bribe had been unnecessary, but he'd rather not take a chance. No power, no elevator, no car. Still he found himself resenting that bribe.

Then he laughed at himself. So he was well–dressed and the guy had made a quick thirty bucks. They had each got what he wanted.

Lex seemed carefree as they sauntered Fifth Avenue, almost like a child in a candy store. It was a bright afternoon, the sun was warm, and they were surrounded by the gaiety of Saturday crowds. She smiled at the world and chattered happily.

He bought her a corsage of violets at a stand near St. Patrick's; a tiny gold pen set at Tiffany's. They walked through Saks, and admired the window display at Steuben's.

He felt smug, satisfied, and very paternal.

INTERLUDE

Violent earthquakes split the Rift Valley, an unpleasant piece of real estate in Africa. They lowered the floor of the Afar depression near Djibouti. Molten rock from depths of sixty to one hundred miles penetrated crevices and cavities, filling the widening gaps in the earth, glowing into the night sky.

Ardoukoba, the low volcano in the Afar area began to spew lava three hundred feet into the air; while from Kilimanjaro's new cone came gas and rumbles. Geysers of sodium bicarbonate, alkali dust, lye, spiraled up from the depths of Lakes Natron and Magadi.

In the United States, salt water began to well up into the deep clefts of Death Valley.

On a mountain in the Smokies a house–sized block of granite, stable for centuries in its damp foundation, turned in the dust now beneath it and rolled down the mountainside.

High in the Catskills big pumps pushed water up hill to run down, powering the giant generators that fed power to the megapolis to the south.

One pump began gulping air. Then another. And another . . .

4

Lex was at the podium.

From the back of the small auditorium under Lincoln Center, Craig looked over the audience to see if he could spot that rather extraneous character of yesterday, Yuri, but if the young man were there he didn't see him.

The lecture was going well. Her audience was listening without a cough or a rustle, but she was getting to a part that worried him, and he concentrated to catch their reaction.

"Time and space are the great opposed polarities," she was saying. "Their reciprocal states pulse the alternating current of the universe . . ."

He had cautioned her about going so deeply into her findings. "You'll lose their attention," he had said. "It's too—it's a bit excessive for us ordinary humans."

She had laughed at him. "You've got to tug a bit at their intelligences," she'd told him. "I'll make this short, but it's something people need to understand, because it's basic to understanding what the electronics they live among is all about."

The audience remained quiescent. He smiled to himself. She was good. She would "tug at their intelligences" as she had said, but would then take them back to more familiar territory, over and over again, until she got her ideas across to those in their secure world of the seen, to whom these were strange and rather forbidding concepts.

And so they listened, trusting her to lead them slowly into an understanding of the invisible and, to them, elusive forces to which they were told they were subject.

He, himself, found it difficult at times to follow what he secretly thought of as her fairy-tale-world of magic and even, perhaps, voodoo.

They listened to her as to an oracle—yet how many of them, in their own world of the seen, have any idea of how vulnerable we of this civilization have made ourselves?

How many of them recognize that if we turned back now, if we put into practice today the measures to correct our depredations, that—we are already too late?

How on God's green earth—not so green any more—could we change things quickly enough to avert physical catastrophe? Stop trashing the earth, and immediately start cleaning her up? Run all cars and trucks on propane? Take half of them off the roads. Put effective scrubbers on all smokestack industries? Switch to co-generation plants using garbage and trash? Find solutions to nuclear waste and storage?

Not in a decade, but now? Over night?

We are already beyond the point of no return, he realized.

Yet the technology can't completely fail, no matter the symptoms. It is too alive, too vibrant, surging ahead with its computers and understandings of causes—yet disregarding the essentials that make our lives possible. Even the oxygen we breathe is depleting.

He had told Lex to look up at the lights which were the city's stars. He, himself, had been looking down into the caverns beneath the city—almost as far below as the city's towers were above. The football field sized caverns where the city was webbed for power; where were the huge tunnels that brought in water.

And what would an earthquake do there? There were eleven faults that he knew of beneath Manhattan itself, little noted and less publicized.

Suddenly his collar felt tight. He wanted to pull off the anachronism of the tie he was wearing. We are as vulnerable as ants building mounds in a dry wash in the dessert of the universe, he told himself; and we very much resemble those busy ants, making paths across the wash, hurrying and scurrying from hither to you.

Lex was continuing. There would be only two or three more sentences before she switched to a lighter tone.

"Time is the great differentiator," she was saying. "Space is the great integrator, The polarity of charged particles is the resultant of this dichotomy. In particles, the tiny center is the electromagnetic element. The space element. The tremendous dielectric—opposed electric—field around and through that center, is the time element.

"You as humans are . . ."

The lights went out. The auditorium was plunged into a blackness so complete it was as if he were blind.

There was a minute of silence as the audience waited for the lights to come back on. Then the rustling began. People were beginning to stand up; to make their way into the aisles.

"Sit still," Craig raised his voice against the beginnings of hubub. "Sit still. This is a safe building. There is nothing wrong other than a short in the lighting system. You are in no danger."

But would they come back on? That, he thought, is the sixty-four dollar question.

He forced his way gently through the people already in the aisles, towards the podium. The steps were on the left, he remembered, found and mounted them. It would not be long before a panic started, unless he could take control.

His eyes were adjusting to the blackness, and he could begin to see the red battery–lit exit signs.

"Lex?" he called quietly, hoping she would hear him over the increasing noise.

"Here," he heard her voice back. He reached her, took her hand in his. Then, making his voice sure and commanding, he said, "We will form a line. I know the way. Mrs. Gallagher and I will lead you out. Take your neighbor's hand. There is no danger."

As the noise began to decrease, he added, "If you get lost from the line, look for the exit signs."

There was a scream from the center of the auditorium. "I dropped my purse! I can't find it!"

"It will be found and returned to you, Madam," Craig shouted as the background became clamorous. "Grab anybody's hand and stay in line."

You can find the way, he told himself with less confidence than he wished, listening to the beginnings of dread behind him.

"It's black as a witches tit," he whispered to Lex. She giggled. It was the reaction he wanted. She began to sing. "Show me the way to go home . . ." Other voices joined and the line moved more easily.

He began to pattern the way in his mind. The cavernous parking areas—he thought back to the way they'd come in, a rather complicated path. He made himself visualize what he knew of the sprawling building. The parking areas would be to the left, he decided; and there would be doors going that way. The eleva-

42

tors they'd come up would not be working. He'd have to find the stairs.

The auditorium was on a lower floor, and probably in line with some of the parking . . .

Slowly, as the line behind the two of them began to take definite form and the hysteria quieted a bit with the singing, he led the snake–like progression through the nearest exit door.

In the hallway there was more hysteria as other auditoriums emptied helter–skelter, other people jostled for a way.

Again and again he shouted his commands. Get in line. Follow. The building is safe. We are going towards the parking areas.

The singing faltered and died, but the line—or was it lines now?—followed. Craig's fingers, dragging along the wall, came finally to elevator doors; and beyond them to a red-lit sign "Stairs." Were they above the parking areas? Parking would be on the lowest floors. Or would he be leading them into a myriad of basements and a losing battle to find their ways between great furnaces and electrical installations?

He'd chance it. Two flights, he decided.

"Hold the railing," he called behind. "Pass the word." The followers had not become docile. He could hear sobs and recriminations. But mostly they held in line behind him, accepting his lead.

At the foot of the first flight, he decided not to try going down further, and led the line through the door there—and into the parking area.

A few cars were already switching on lights; hardy souls who had found not only the parking, but their own vehicles to which they had keys. They could see again, if not well, at least there was something of comfort.

A motor started.

Beyond this I will have no control, he told himself. Beyond this, these people will have to find their own way.

"All right," he called. "You can see a bit now. You can find a way."

Whether he was heard he did not know, but he hardened his grip on Lex's hand and pulled her fast through. Any direction, he told himself. We'll find a way out of here.

43

Behind Lex a rather elderly couple held on, though as far as he could tell they'd left the others behind.

Just behind them a car began to pull out. He let go of Lex's hand and turned in front of it. The driver almost failed to stop, but he held his place in front of the headlights.

"These are decent people." he shouted to the driver who was hesitating to lower his window to talk. "They've been attending a lecture." He looked at the couple with Lex. The man was gray-haired, pale in the headlights; the woman disheveled. "Take these two to a safe place where they can get a taxi."

Reluctantly, the man lowered the window a fraction. "The car is full," he said bitterly. "We are four people."

Craig's voice assumed authority. "You can take two more. This is an emergency." He grabbed the back door handle. For a minute he thought the driver would pull ahead, but a woman in back reached to the door lock and pulled it up. "We'll take them," she said in a quiet voice, and Craig shepherded the two in.

"What about you two?" the woman asked, but the driver slammed the car into gear and started it moving. The four in back were still maneuvering, and fell into a heap. Lex jumped out of the way.

There were more cars moving now, and Craig waited until one stopped.

"Where are you two going?"

It was a well dressed couple, fairly young, and Craig made his voice gracious.

"To wherever we can get a taxi," he said. "We'd be delighted to ride with you, if you will."

The back door opened to his hand as the driver released the lock.

"You may have trouble getting a taxi," the young driver said. His voice was scared but even. "Where are you going?"

"The other side of the Park," Craig told him. "Central Park East at 65th."

"We'll take you." Then the voice spilled over. The driver, about twenty Craig guessed, was full of adrenalin and needed to talk.

"Lord," he said. "I've never been so scared. People were screaming. Doris, though," he gestured toward the girl, "she was

44

great. Held my hand . . . and . . . well, I saw the exit lights and we . . . well, we got out."

"It wasn't a real emergency," Craig said quietly. "The building was safe. It was just the lights." Then he was ashamed of himself. The youngster needed to have been a hero rescuing his lady. Little enough chance for that, these days. We tend to recognize the maternal instinct in women, but we forget that a man needs to be the protector, and it's just as deep a need. Both instincts are being lost, he thought, for better or worse.

It was Doris herself who rescued him. "Tom kept his head," she told them. "He kept falling over people, but he got us out. It was—it was really something. Everybody crying and shouting. But Tom kept his head," she ended proudly.

Good gal, Craig thought. That's what your Tom needs. Pride. Encouragement. And he'll be needing it more for the next few days anyhow.

The streets were a river of headlights below the dark buildings. All traffic lights were out. It was eerie as their hosts took them through the Park and let them out in front of their building.

The street was clogged with vehicles, people dodging between them; the buildings dark shadows above.

Craig started to pull out his keys. The doorman was gone. To his wife and family?

Lex reached for his arm as he started to the door of the lobby. "Craig? Our car is packed? Do we have to go back up—four floors in the pitch dark? And then find our own door? Craig? Can't we just get our car and go?"

"Your next lecture? The publisher's party?" His voice was almost debonair with relief. He knew the answer, but did she?

"There won't be another," she said firmly. "You were right. The party's off. Even if the lights come back on, people will be scared."

He tucked her hand under his arm. The headlights made the tall dark buildings above them seem more menacing than before.

He began forcing their way through the crowds—not panicked, but verging, across 68th to Lexington, up Lexington towards the ramp garage, thanking his stars that the car was not locked behind an elevator that would not be working.

They neared a nearly stationary glut of police cars, ambulances and people, lit by the red and white lights of the emergency vehicles. A subway entrance. He felt Lex catch her breath as he pulled her into the street, around the scene. Police were there, shepherding people out—bedraggled people, some bleeding. He could see them—trainloads of people on narrow walkways beside the subway tracks, with only the lights of such flashlights as the guards might have had. The women mostly teetering on high heels. There was an undercurrent of the sound of grief and moans. Someone was vomiting quietly into a gutter.

They've walked the narrow path beside the rails in the dark, stumbling and frightened, from wherever the trains stopped, he thought; and there are other trainloads behind them.

There was a stench in the air. It was still there when they were well past the subway entrance and its victims.

The stench of terror, he realized. It would cling to the streets for a good long while, and would remain in the subconscious longer.

Lex was clutching his arm in a vicelike grip.

"There's nothing we can do," he told her softly. "The problem's too big, too complex, for anything other than organized services."

"But—there will be people in elevators . . .?"

"Do you have any idea how even to begin getting people out of elevators—in the pitch black dark? You'd be more hindrance than help."

Her hand relaxed. Her chin went up. By the time they reached the garage, her stride was purposeful. But as they got into their car, he saw the tears coursing down her cheeks.

"Do you have your press card with you?" he asked gruffly.

She nodded.

As he started the car he felt the cold controls settle over him, the controls he'd learned in the war; as he'd felt them on the flight deck of the carrier when his plane had landed safely, and the one behind missed the cable . . . Cold, ready to take the air again, because that was what he was there for.

INTERLUDE

On the seventeenth floor of One Park Avenue a rather dowdy young woman was at work at a computer terminal. As far as she knew, she was the only one left in the offices tonight, and it was not happy–making, but the figures had to be in the computer by morning.

It was miserable work. Figures. Column after column, but it had to be done. She wasn't young enough for this any more, she told herself. Twenty–six and with a three year old child waiting with an elderly neighbor. She ought to be home with him. She ought to be anywhere but in this big barn of a place, alone, and, she admitted, scared.

Abruptly the lights went out.

She shivered, then laughed lightly at herself. This would give her a five minute break.

She fished around her desk until she found her cigarettes, lit one. The tiny flame of the lighter broke the stygian darkness for a second, making her feel more secure. She began thinking over the work remaining. Not so much now, but she could be getting it organized in her mind.

The cigarette was down to the filter before she stubbed it out, and still no lights.

She found her bag and felt through it for the penlight she always carried. With its tiny gleam she made her way through the sur–rounding desks to the doorway.

It wasn't much light, and the desks and walls seemed to take new positions as she passed them, but she got across the hall and into the boss's office, where there was a window.

Blackness had replaced the golden glow of New York's evening. Black–out, she thought, but as she pressed her nose against the window she could see—far up Park Avenue—a building with amber lights. And across, probably beyond Madison, another. Not the usual brightness, but at least subdued lights. Generators?

She looked down—and down and down and down—but it was too dark to see the street below, only the reflections of headlights.

Her fingers gripped the window sill. The seventeenth floor, and the elevators wouldn't be working.

She could wait for lights to come back on, as surely they would? She could wait—but she had heard of the great East Coast blackout in '64. Fourteen hours it had been that time.

She shuddered, then shrugged. At least she'd be going down, not up, and that shouldn't be too terrible.

She worked her way slowly back to her desk, smothering a rising fear; found her jacket, picked up her bag. This will be an adventure she told herself firmly.

It took a while to find the door to the stairs in the now terrifying maze of offices and desks and lobby. Even with the penlight, the normally familiar rooms took on strange patterns.

The stairs themselves were pitch black, the cement steps sharp and hard. She clung to the iron hand rail. The penlight barely lit a few steps below, and at the corners where the stairs turned she found herself sliding her feet along, feeling for the next steps.

At least I can't see down the stairwell, she thought. It just might scare the pants off me.

She had managed two flights when she heard voices, and barely kept herself from crying out in relief. She stood still while she got her voice under control, then called down: "Hi, below! I have a pen light if you would like to wait for me!"

There were four of them, and the comfort of being among people again was an almost dizzying relief. One young girl, an older woman, and two middle aged men, one with a paunch.

The backs of her legs were already aching, and she realized that high heels—even the medium high heels she wore—were not for mountain climbing, up or down.

"If you're wearing heels," she told the other women, "let's take them off and carry them. We've still thirteen floors to go." Briefly she thought of her panty–hose and dismissed the thought.

At first there was excited conversation, but as they inched downward it dried up. By the time they reached the eighth floor (or had she lost count?) her legs were shaking with the strain, and she declared a rest stop. Since she had the tiny light (how long will it last?) they obeyed.

By the fifth floor, they heard more voices below, and the parade down the stairs took on a more jovial atmosphere. Aching legs or not, the stair well no longer seemed so horrifying.

Tonight I shall take a taxi home, she assured herself.

As they reached the lobby—where was the guard who normally checked people in and out?—the whole adventure seemed a gay affair, and they were laughing about mountain climbing in Manhattan. Skis we should have, one young man said happily (he'd come on at the fourth floor.)

"And a ski lift," she'd answered, determined not to feel the exhaustion that was making her whole body shake.

She put on her heels and they went into Park Avenue. Automobiles and trucks were making the street itself at least lighter, but overhead the buildings loomed, ominous in their darkness.

There were taxis, and they all waved valiantly, staying in a group; but the taxis were full, crammed, every one.

It was a very long time before she decided that to get to her apartment on East 13th—and to her son with the elderly neighbor in the next apartment—she would have to walk. There was no thought of the usual subway. There would be no subway. She had a brief moment of thankfulness that the blackness had not caught her on one.

She felt in her bag for the tube of mace that was always there.

"Anybody going my way?" she asked, but the others were off in different directions. There'd be no taxis at all, down through the East side, and it wasn't an area you'd choose to stroll through, even in the day time. Even at night with lights.

She set off resolutely. How many blocks to a mile? She'd heard eight of the short blocks, or four of the long ones between the avenues.

She'd be going through the Kleins block, blacked out and available to looters—no, she'd go a couple of blocks East before she got there.

A newspaper kiosk was open, and she stopped beside it for company, leaning against its wall, smiling at the man behind his shelf of papers. Passing cars gave enough light so that the almost-terror of the blacked-out stairs was not a factor, but her exhaustion was.

There was a jam-up in the street at Park and 23rd, and an empty taxi caught in it. She ran to it, forcing her rubbery legs. She pulled on the door, but it was locked.

The cabby looked at her kindly. "Lady," he said "there's no more gas. I gotta get home while I still can. They can't pump gas without electricity." The jam broke and he drove off.

Home, she thought. The tiny apartment, blacked out, with almost no water—but with Tommy's warm arms around her, and Mrs. Blossom next door. A beacon.

Ahead of her, a dark mass of huddled forms. She cringed, wanting to hide. A car came by, and it was only a pile of garbage bags.

She felt a scream rising in her throat, and began to run . . . .

He was eleven. Daddy had been gone for a week now, and he wasn't at all sure Daddy would be back. There had been harsh words and violence when he left.

The babies were screaming, and the smell was awful. There wasn't enough water to keep them clean, and they couldn't even flush the toilet—perhaps once or twice a day. The new baby would be coming pretty soon, and there was no money to . . . to . . . anything.

When the lights went out, something inside cracked wide open.

"Momma," he cried over the babies' screams, "I'm gonna get some money."

She was sobbing. She didn't answer, or he didn't hear her. He found the door to the apartment. That wasn't hard. He'd lived here a year, and he knew it inside out. The stairs were no problem either. So you couldn't see. He wished he couldn't hear—or smell.

Almost as though he could see, he dived down the five floors, taking the steps two at a time. No acrobatics, though. This time it was serious.

There was a little light on the streets. Cars. And lots of people.

The bar next door. Somebody was pushing the last of the drunks out, and the door was still open a crack.

He slouched against the door, forcing his way under the arms of whoever it was pushing it closed.

"Pops," he said gruff as he could make his voice, "where's the money? I've gotta gun, and I'll use it."

The shot took him in the stomach, and with a whoosh he fell back against the door, closing it.

The last thing he heard was a voice saying, "Get the body at least a block away. Quick. I'll hold on here."

He stood at a window on the forty-seventh floor, looking down over the buildings that hid Battery Park, towards Staten Island. The Statue of Liberty with its point of light was a tiny figure against the dark waters.

He'd said he needed time to think over the proposition he'd just been offered. Actually he'd stalled to give himself time to figure how to handle it most profitably for himself.

Two of the others wanted to go along, but he'd nix that. He'd take his staff, but it would be a lone ranger job. Give himself a free hand to manage the deals to his liking.

China had suddenly become an open opportunity, and he'd been asked to head a consortium that planned to fill the vacuum.

The massacre of the students—20,000 he'd heard—had scared foreign money the hell out of that country. Did people think that was the only massacre in the world these days? Or any other days, for that matter. Human rights was a coward's term.

But the money had fled. The media P. R. had been too much for the business community. So now there was that vacuum, and a vacuum meant money to be made.

What would the damn commies in the saddle be like now? Bullies, of course, but cold cash would settle that. It was one huge bastard of a market.

He smiled to himself.

Yes, he'd head the consortium that was asking him to go, and he'd go with his own cash as well as theirs.

Millions, they'd bring out. Billions.

So he didn't speak Chinese. He knew the Chinese—done business with them over here. Hard-nosed, but they liked the almighty dollar, and it would be cash he'd be offering.

The Chinks would just have to speak English. The power brokers wanting to make deals, a chunk of which would go into their own pockets, would damn well speak English. Money would do his talking for him. Bribes? That was just good business.

He turned towards the fax machine in the corner, and as he did the lights went out; the telex in another corner stopped its low hum

51

For Christ's sake, he thought, and in the darkness, alleviated only a little by the big night–dark windows behind him, made his way to the desk and picked up the right–hand phone.

Only silence from the receiver.

"Miss Stance!" he called, then realized that it was late and he'd sent her along home.

He made his way through the door to the blackness of her inner office, finally found the contraption on her desk that put him, through her, in touch with the inner and outer worlds. There were no lights on the instrument—of course, he told himself, but push buttons as he would he could get no sound from the receiver.

With the thought of other offices and other telephones, he started towards the hallway, then realized he hadn't looked to see how widespread the problem might be. He finally found the door back into his own office, and the window.

The great buildings of the Wall Street area loomed like huddled beasts, dark and ominous. Not a light was showing, though out on the river he could see boats, lighted and free.

I might as well relax for a bit, he decided, and made his way to the cabinet that held his small bar. By feel and familiarity he found and poured Scotch into a glass, filled it with ice cubes, and turned on the tap for a splash of water. There was a gurgle of air going into the pipes from the opened faucet, and he stared in its direction. *Of course. At this height, water would be pumped and—no pumps.*

That was when the stillness around him sank into his consciousness. The hum of the telex was gone. The water was gone. Even the whisper of air as it pumped through this air–tight building—that, too, was gone.

He raised the Scotch to his lips, his hand trembling just a bit.

5

While the car warmed up, Craig shucked his tie, opened his collar, fastened his seat-belt, then checked to see that Lex was belted in and the doors locked.

"Our pint-sized tank," he told her with a grim smile, "with which we will make our escape from this madhouse."

He didn't fool himself that it would be easy. They had come through the packed streets, watched panic start and grow. His little Tercel was no match for the big cars, or for the trucks and semi's that would be a major part of the throng; but it was light on its feet and could dodge.

He drove slowly down the ramps, trying to get a glimpse of what was happening below, but without success.

As they reached the exit to Lexington Avenue, he realized that panic was not just well underway, it was in full flood. The Avenue was filled with people and vehicles of all kinds, and it took him several minutes to squeeze into an opening, even on a right turn.

This wasn't just fear of a blackout. This was a cumulative fear; a fear that had started with low water, bringing on distrust of the system, and that hit crisis with the disappearance of power.

This was not to be compared with the 1964 blackout. This was the era of drugs and triple and quadruple locks on every door. This was the time when you didn't walk the streets at night; when you feared for your life and safety under "normal" circumstances. These were the years when you lived daily on the edge of terror. This was the time of gang rapes and senseless murders. The year when one out of every four households had already been victimized by crime, when each person feared he would be next . . .

. . . When frustration was the daily gridlock; with helplessness of every kind; when terrorists held a club over every head; when nuclear plants were known to be verging on meltdown; when confrontation and war brought the potential of nuclear winter very near.

Perhaps the symptoms we should have watched were the English soccer crowds when just plain people with no real provocation, stampeded and killed each other? Or death threats to a tennis player? Or bombs to civil rights advocates?

When frustration and dread are all pervasive, he told himself, madness lies just beneath the surface.

He kept his face calm. Let Lex do the analyzing and the drawing of conclusions. His job was to get them out of this hell without an accident that would disable their car, leaving them—he shuddered—on foot.

He turned East. "We'll get over to the East River Drive," he told her. "Take it to the Cross Bronx and the George Washington Bridge. Get off Manhattan as quickly as possible. The blackout may go into New Jersey, but at least we'll be off the island, free to move in any direction. The first thing is to get off Manhattan itself."

"The Lincoln Tunnel might be less crowded?" Her voice was strained.

He turned his head quickly to look at her, and as quickly back to the hazards of the turmoil in the street.

"Do you want," he asked, keeping his voice as relaxed as possible but hearing its tensions, "Do you want to be in the Tunnel when the air blowers are not working? When the exhaust from those cars has nowhere to go except into your lungs? Have you any idea how much air is pumped through those tunnels at all times, to keep people from being asphyxiated? The blowers will not be working."

"Oh." It was a small voice, and he knew he had been hard on her. But for God's sake . . . He made his shoulders relax, putting his attention back on the problems before him, working towards the right so he could turn right towards Second Avenue.

When they finally came within sight of the Drive he caught his breath. Gridlock. In both directions. Cars bumper to bumper, standing still.

For the first time it occurred to him that they might not be able to get off the island; that they might be huddled in an overall gridlock that could not be untangled; their car hopelessly cemented in this mass of steel and exhaust.

He reached over to pat Lex's knee. "We'll make it, Love. This isn't the end of the world. There are remnants of civilization left, even here." But not on the East River Drive, he added to himself.

Without traffic lights, the corner was jammed, vehicles forcing into the intersection from four directions—and he was trying a left turn! Then there was a bare opening on the left, and he slammed his way into it, just as a car came from across the way at full acceleration. It swung against his rear fender, and kept on across behind them.

"Bastard," he muttered; but knew he'd been as bastardly to get around that corner. There was an opening ahead, going up Second Avenue, and he was able to gun the car.

The buildings were brownstone fronts, small stores, and warehouses. Cars and trucks were parked in close procession on both sides of the street, barely leaving two lanes for movement.

He maneuvered into the left lane. He'd be turning left when he could. On any street. He thought they were probably into the one hundreds—probably near 112th—but there was no way he could see the street signs.

More people were swarming into the streets, and the sounds from the cars and trucks and people condensed into a low growl; a hideous growl; a growl that was growing as the minutes passed.

He saw a man throw a board against a plate glass store front; and when it didn't break pick up the board and use it as a battering ram. He saw grocery carts loaded with loot being rushed down the street.

They were inching towards an intersection when ahead he saw fire pouring from the windows of a building. As he watched, as they neared it at a snail's pace, the vacuum at the bottom opened, and the building torched, adding the full-throated roar of a devastating blow torch to the anarchy of the scene.

The corner was near, nearly blocked, but he threw their car into a violent left turn, barely missing being run down by a huge truck, cutting off a motorcycle that was using its size to wind between the farrago of vehicles, each packed with people.

More brownstones; more warehouses; more storefronts of small shops; more looting.

A huge man, crowbar in hand, tried to insert it into the door on Lex's side as they were blockaded to a stop. Craig swung the car through an opening that should have been too small, scraping both sides, and ground on.

There was a small, smothered whimper from beside him. "He wanted the car, not you," Craig's voice was rough. Then he grinned. "He might have taken you as lagniappe," he said in the lightest tone he could manage.

"Oh, Craig! These are human beings! Normally sane people!" He could hear the horror and the fascination in her voice. She was repelled as an individual, enthralled as an anthropologist, and flooded with adrenalin by the danger. He felt the same, underneath his cold control but had to keep the calm veneer, dared not take his attention off the street.

"It's still individual action," he said. "Each person for himself. The mobs will come later. That's when there are no people left, only animal–mobs."

His face was set. "It's when the mobs form," he told her, "the mindless mobs that find a leader, that translates fear and hopelessness into anger and destruction. That's when it gets vicious. Wholesale, wanton destruction . . ."

Mobs. If this continued another twenty–four, thirty–six hours they would form of themselves. Powerful. Mindless. Primitive. Huge dinosaurs made up of individual bodies, wasting, destroying, without purpose except a lust for revenge. Against what? Against "them." Against all powerlessness that each individual had felt his life long. An animal urge to dominate, to mutilate, to charge over a mountain of bodies and tear down the walls that had imprisoned them.

Yes, unless this was brought under control, and quickly, the mobs would form.

* * *

It was a nightmare of fender–benders and full–sized wrecks. He used his bumper to clear a car, deserted in the middle of the street, shoving it with a crash into a parked car so that he could get through.

At Nicholas Avenue, it was a right turn, and he managed it, past the University where students—he assumed they were students—seemed to be as thoroughly deranged, adding to the wreckage and violence, as the throngs they had already passed through.

They were finally at the Medical Center, had reached the entry ramp to the Cross Bronx, were on it, moving slowly up the ramp to its top . . .

A squad of soldiers materialized, one uniformed youngster running in front of them, waving them to a halt.

Before Craig could try to stop her, Lex pulled up on the lock on her door and threw herself from the car, heading for the soldier as she searched her bag. She came up triumphantly with her Press card, and waved it before him.

"Press" she shouted. "I've got to get through!"

Craig could hear the soldier's voice—National Guard?—over the growls of the surroundings. "You gotta wait here. We've got an Army Convoy comin' in." He looked so young.

Lex gathered her tiny form into a military stance. He could hear her put authority and anger into her voice. "I've got to get the story out!" She looked so tiny and intrepid. "Nobody knows what's happening. Press!" she said with the fierceness of a bantam rooster facing down a marauder.

"Everybody's got to get through. They're running like ants." But he could hear the softening of the soldier's tone, and saw his slight smile as he looked at the trim figure of his antagonist, dressed for a lecture and only slightly dishevelled. Then he shrugged. "I guess one more won't hurt. But you'll play hell getting across the bridge."

He held up his hand to stop the next car moving towards the bridge, making a space for theirs.

"Good girl," was Craig's only comment as she flung herself, breathless, back into the car.

"I packed my lap top. We do have the story, and I'll write it," she told him, and subsided meekly. Then, in a small voice, "and I have another chapter of Electronic Anthropology . . ."

The sun was rising by the time they got onto the George Washington Bridge itself. It was almost night again as they finally reached beyond Newark, beyond Westfield, beyond the vast snail of traffic, watching convoys of army vehicles moving into the cities as they moved at less than a turtle's pace, out.

"Take the first motel that doesn't have a `no,'" he heard her command. "We've got a story every newspaper in the land will want."

"Give me a couple of hours before you go on television," he told her in exasperation, worn out, slumping at the wheel, but strangely jubilant.

At the motel he shucked his clothes and fell into bed, as she set up her lap top and began to concentrate.

They'd escaped. His instinct to pack the car first and to move it to a ramp garage had been sound.

Prescient, he told himself as he fell asleep.

57

INTERLUDE

There were five men and a woman gathered in the safe house in France.

The woman was gaunt. Her long hair was drawn back from an olive-skinned face, twisted high on her head. It was a long face with a prominent chin, and deep-set black eyes. She was tall, though not so tall as to command attention. Skeletal would be the word.

She had been called "Bones" as a child, adopted it as her name, and had been called by that name in almost every language of the world.

Her voice was soft, educated. She wore tailored slacks and shirt with the grace of a model as she strode up and down the room before them . . . until you noticed the twisted hand, the crick of a neck that wouldn't quite come straight.

The five men were nondescript, sinuous, stringy. As feral as herself. Her tribe. Her commandos. Hers. As though long association had imprinted on them her own characteristics, they resembled her, each one, in tilt of head, in expression, in movement.

In her hand Bones held a package of what looked to be three tennis balls, silicone-plasticked against a piece of cardboard. The plastic vacuumed tightly around the balls, and around the cardboard as well.

"Are you functional yet?" she asked one of them. "Are you in condition to work?"

"I gotta work, Bones. I gotta get back. Every time I get the shakes I remember that fat-assed sadist with the tongs, taking his pleasure in every scream. Getting an orgasm when I spasmed. I don't walk too good yet, but I can get around. And I've got a way to keep myself from crying."

She nodded. These were things she understood.

"We were too long getting you out," she said gently. "But at least you're off the lists. The records say you're dead."

"Don't count me out. I . . . well, I gotta get even."

"You'll be in," she said. "You'll be in up to your eyeballs. And this time . . . this time . . . this time . . . ."

Then her voice became a whiplash. "The Iraqis," she said, "tried to take out the Kurds with chemical warfare. So they killed a few

*hundred Kurds, and nobody cared. Called it the poor man's atom
bomb. And passed laws.*

*"We've got here," and she held up the tennis balls, "We've got .
. ." she paused for effect. "We've got the poor man's hydrogen bomb."*

*They watched her wordlessly. They had learned early, when
she'd first gathered them together as her personal team, not to
interrupt. She was the Boss. She was Bones. You listened. She had
education. She had inherited money. And—she had brains.*

*In her face was the naked hate–filled asceticism of terrorism; the
addictive orgasm of the act of laying waste.*

*How she—the daughter of wealth—had come to this they none
of them knew. She had herself blocked out the childhood beatings
and sexual abuse and fear; the helplessness of being subjected not
only to her father's rage, but to his friends' aberrations and desires.*

*Her troop knew themselves to be dregs. Her violence they did not
understand, nor try to. She was Bones. The leader. The brains.*

*"Always before," she told them, "the bombs and the kidnappings
and hi–jackings to get the attention of the world—people forgot. One
day sensations. Things that happened to somebody else.*

*"If you want to bring the world to its knees—there has to be
terror. Real terror."*

Her face lit with an orgiastic joy.

*"If you want to create the breakdown of the system, we must
make a situation in which every human being is panicked. Men,
women and children, trembling for their lives.*

*"We," she said, stroking the package she held lovingly, "must
wipe them out until the few that are left come begging to us."*

*She looked in triumph at her cohorts. She had their attention
and the adulation she drank like wine.*

*She held up the card of tennis balls; a child savoring its revenge;
a cat ready to spring on its prey; a god, casting his thunderbolts on
a disobedient people, glorying in his power.*

*"These," she said, "contain a concentration of viruses more
powerful than any yet known. Once the virus enters the human
system, it remains quiet for several weeks—and highly contagious.
After that, death is inevitable within another week. It paralyzes the
muscles of the body. All the muscles. Inside and out.*

"These look like tennis balls," she said. "They contain the product of the most secret laboratory in the world—and, it lies in the United States of America.

"Once this package is opened—and I have a hundred of these packages—once it is opened, once the air touches the ... " she grinned, and the grin was that of a skull ... "Once the air touches these tennis balls, they disintegrate, and the virus is freed.

"The first symptoms are like flu. The second symptoms are paralysis. The third is death. But meantime, for the weeks of incubation, each carrier will have infected almost every person with whom he comes in contact. And each of them will infect his contacts ..."

This was terrorism at its most lethal, and those in the room were filled with her passion.

She looked at each of them in turn, her eyes burning with the fierceness of her pride. "You will take these packages into the waiting rooms of the airline terminals of the world. Just as your plane is called, you will split a package open and let the balls roll, as if by accident, under chairs and into corners.

"It will take about five minutes for the casing of each ball to disintegrate, and you will already be airborne, on your way to your next terminal. Your tickets and destinations are ready.

"When you have fulfilled your missions, you will make your way to this island." She held up a map. "Off Lybia. After we get there, no one will be allowed on or off.

"The epidemic will last about six months. Within a year we can come out of hiding safely."

They would not, she knew, escape the virus themselves. But that fact they did not need to know. She would be in the home she had inherited on an island off the coast of Africa, where she could prevent anybody—anybody at all—from coming or going.

6

They were on the highway headed towards the Shenandoah Valley.

Craig's mind shuddered away from the horrors behind. The past two days seemed unreal, a fantasy. Like leaving a movie set after a particularly ghastly take.

The sound effects had been turned off. The all-pervasive animal growl was gone. The camera men had climbed down from their perches. The grips had packed their tools. The extras who made up the mad scenes of disaster were returning their costumes to the warehouse of wardrobes. The set for the burning building was being torn down.

The last barked instructions of the director seemed to ring in his ears: "Next scene: The couple rides off into the sunset. Craig kisses his horse."

Well, the sound effects weren't quite turned off, he decided as a huge tractor-trailer growled up beside him and passed.

Suddenly a shout of laughter escaped his throat. Beside him Lex came awake with a start.

"We made it!" Then his voice calmed. "We're out and on our way," he said.

She smiled contentedly and leaned back again in her seat.

He needed to talk. In spite of hours of sleep, the adrenalin in his system was high.

"It wasn't a very good gamble, our getting out," he said, almost conversationally. "We could have been left on foot. We could have been caught into the madhouse and injured—or killed."

"You got us out. I knew you would."

"It was like being caught behind enemy lines in a war," he said. "It was like . . . We had half a tub of water, and candles and enough food at home. It may have been a foolish gamble. The odds were stacked against us."

The scenes of their escape were flashing through his mind now. Maybe they'd been right, maybe wrong. But unless power and water were restored almost overnight to the city—how long would it have taken for the insanity to reach them? Their building?

Always before, riots and panic had been confined to the ghettos, to the drug–infested areas. But those areas had grown— and crack, and the new home–made drug, crank, created an insanity so vicious that it was a new thing.

No longer were they what Lex called the "upstairs people" isolated and immune in their comforts. Not when the mobs of the dispossessed showed the rampaging thirst of the hopeless.

It had actually been a poor gamble, trying to get out. The chances were high they'd be wrecked and on foot before they had gotten past the building that had torched. He remembered it as they had approached in the chaos New York had become; re-membered watching it torch. For minutes, as they had edged nearer, just small fires bursting through windows. Then the vac-uum at the base had opened and the fires roared together—a blow torch in action; one single flaming pyre from street to rooftop, roaring like an express train.

A heavy gust of wind shook the car. Automatically he flexed the wheels to counter the effect.

When the building torched, they had been near a corner, and had been able to turn away. Still in the crush; still part of the panic; but away from the sparks and flying debris that would light other buildings.

If they'd stayed, how long would the Upstairs people be safe in their comforts? Depending on how soon water and power could be turned on. Depending on how much savvy the viciousness of drugs left their users. Depending on how soon the army would become effective; how much water their trucks could bring in.

Depending on how much more of the intricate infrastructure that maintained a megapolis felt the stress and began to crumble.

A second gust of wind shook not only his car but the tractor-trailer ahead, swaying it dangerously. Then a third gust.

He pushed on the accelerator and passed the monster ahead, then kept his speed and went three cars beyond, before pulling in behind a pickup.

Tornado? This was not a normal wind. Its power had nearly lifted their wheels from the road.

The weather. Was it really changing? He'd scoffed at people who had said it was. Told them they just didn't remember. Had he been wrong? Was this, too, a major factor? Weather becoming increasingly violent?

Water and power. Was the violence of the weather another factor in the gamble of their leaving? Was it another small fire in a window of the building? Not just of a city, but a nation?

Was the mad director of the mad movie conjuring up really vast special effects for the entertainment of the gods?

The brush–fire wars across the world; the insurgents fighting in almost every nation; the contras and the entrenched armies murdering peoples without real rhyme or reason? Ethnic cleansing? In this country the strikes, the marches. All with fists waving in the breeze and palpable hatred coming through from the screens that watched their every movement. "Pick a cause and march," "Pick a cause and destroy." "Pick a cause . . ." and hate.

Were they, too, elements of the crumbling of an infra–structure—not just of a city, but of a planet? Would they, too, create a vacuum at their base and roar together to torch into a single, overwhelming holocaust?

The car was shaking steadily now, like a bone in the jaw of a monster. Ahead of him the canvas that had covered the back of the pickup tore loose, banged against his windshield blinding him briefly, then blew back over his head and was gone. The wind was a tempest that made him keep the wheel canted slightly to the left, forcing his way into the turbulence that was wrenching them to the right.

This was not just a wind. It was a hurricane of wind, without the hurricane of rain. Off the highway trees were tossing and swaying, some bent nearly to the ground. A huge branch tore loose and skittered against a Lincoln ahead of him, pushing the car into the median. The other cars rolled past without stopping, a river of cars, each fighting the wind, but none slowing.

He debated pulling off the road until it subsided, but the thought of the trees swaying towards the highway, of the huge semi behind him oscillating in the wind, tires clutching at the pavement and creeping up to pass him, made the decision. If he kept moving he could dodge. Beside the highway he would be a sitting duck.

He gripped the wheel, keeping as much space as possible between himself and surrounding traffic. They were nearing a city, and the highway opened from two lanes to three, the crush of traffic increasing rapidly to fill all lanes, moving at the same rash pace in defiance of the hurricane of air that swept them. He saw a car ahead blown into the median. He watched several wind–bumped into scraping fenders. But they kept going.

Is everyone crazy? he asked himself; but he had to keep the pace or be run down by the swaying, skittish traffic. This is insane!

As suddenly as it had come, the hurricane of wind stopped. It was as though there had been no turmoil of nature impinging itself on the frantic pace of normal life on the thruway. There were small wrecks along the roadsides, but nothing spectacular.

He drew a deep breath. They were passing the last of the city exits now. It was still three lanes to a side, but dwindled to two before he found his nerves quieting. The tensions would last a while, but for now he could relax.

He reached in his pocket, found a cigar, lit it. It tasted as good as the first cigar of the day; and it was a handle on familiarity.

Lex had gone back to sleep. The fact amazed him. The shaking had been tremendous, but her face was peaceful.

Ahead, traffic was slowing to a stop. He could see the lines of stopped vehicles as far as eye could reach across a small rise in the distance.

An ocean of wind invisibly pounding their asphalt shore could not stop the speeding along the ant–trail that was a thruway, but an obstruction on the highway—probably not even a great one— could hold it immobile for hours.

He pulled to the left lane, geared down and came to a halt a good fifteen feet behind a station wagon.

Lex stirred and sat up. The car might shake and dodge, but as long as it was in motion, she could sleep. Stopped, she waked instantly. It was a phenomena he'd think about—later.

"Grid lock," he told her briefly.

"Where are we?"

"On I–78. Going west towards Easton, Pennsylvania. We're still in New Jersey."

"We may be hours."

"Probably would, if we stayed here. Get out the map and see how far back we have to go to find a side road around this area. I'm going to walk across the median, see if they have too big a culvert in the middle to cross."

She giggled. "They won't like it."

64

"We won't like sitting here hour after hour."

He got out and walked to the center of the median, came back and started the car. "Hooray for four-wheel drive," he said. "Hold onto your hat."

He swung them down the steep bank, bumped through the small culvert at the bottom, and up the other side, where he turned back into the new direction of traffic.

He looked back. No one was following his lead across the median. The cars simply sat.

It felt like an adventure now. He felt as though he'd taken charge again—no longer subject to the vagaries of humans and weather, but in command of his own being and future.

Lex was talking. "Are we in a hurry?" she asked.

"Not now. Maybe later."

"That young man—Yuri—he lives near what he called the Three Corners. Where New York State, New Jersey and Pennsylvania meet. We could stop by on the way. Jeff and Terry aren't expecting us for a few days yet."

"On the way?" His voice was barely sarcastic. "Say a hundred miles north—then a hundred back?"

"We could get off this damned highway. Back where it intersects 206. That's marked in red. It'll be fairly good but not a thruway. Then we sort of wander around until we find him. He said we could come."

He laughed. "You want to find out about his electronic blizzard."

"I want to get out of the prehistoric," she said, smiling happily. "What is this DEM stuff that's worse than the A- Bomb? We've lived under the Bomb so long, we've almost forgotten it's there. He says there's something worse. That we're living under without even knowing about it.

"Anyhow, we need to get out of the catastrophic woods. To talk. To think about other things than . . . than . . . I keep wanting to burst into tears about all the people who can't get out. Let's look away. Get perspective."

He nodded. There was no reason not to take a side-trip. Not that he knew of, he added distrustfully to himself. It would be out of the megapolis, though not far out. Or is there a far enough out, he wondered?

They phoned when they reached the turn-off to 206. It was a gruff voice that answered, but not uncordial.

"You weren't at the last lecture when the lights went out" Lex asked.

"Nope. I'd already.heard enough. You were good, but not that good."

Lex laughed. This boom generation was different. Unyielding, for better or worse. The intelligent ones— and this one seemed intelligent—and the hoodlums; and never the twain shall meet. But they're both—recalcitrant.

"It got quite exciting," was all she said.

"I read about the blackout. Did you get back to your place okay?"

"We got out of the city instead."

"Good thinking."

"We're near your place. May we come over?"

"Yeah, well, I guess so. Come on."

"Be a couple of hours."

"Okay."

"Fractious youngster," Lex remarked dryly as she got back in the car. "I'm glad we've dressed compatibly in slacks and loafers. He might not have let us in."

It took longer than the two hours. The high winds came again. There were branches scattered on the road. They passed a couple of fender-benders, but nothing serious.

They reached the turn-off towards his drive, saw flames coming from a clapboard house on a hill. As they neared it, Craig looked at the sketch map in his lap, looked at the house in amazement. It was Yuri's. The fire looked already beyond control.

He stopped their car far enough back to be safe, and they ran towards the conflagration. Yuri came boiling out, what looked like a huge computer in his arms.

"Get the electronic gear out!" he yelled at them, deposited his load and headed back.

There was no furniture in the living room, only benches and arrays of electronic equipment, with chairs in front of some. An oscilloscope Craig recognized. The rest looked like computers to

66

him, of various sizes, mostly with screens. Printouts were spilling from some. There were files ad infinitum; hand–held measuring devices. One bench of soldering equipment. Vices. Wires. Batteries.

Lex was unplugging and grabbing up the oscilloscope, about as much as she could carry, but she picked up an O–meter and set it on top before heading for the door. Craig took one of the larger instruments.

They ran to a spot under a ham radio tower, where Yuri had put several pieces of the equipment, and turned back as a tank fire truck drove up. Men boiled from it carrying hoses.

"Don't get water in the living room—the fire hasn't reached there yet," Yuri shouted. "My stuff's in there . . . ."

One of the men grinned at him and nodded.

Lex and Craig headed back for the house. "Keep out of the way," one of the firemen told them gruffly. They ignored him, went back for more.

It took only a short while to get the fire under control, but the whole back of the house was a shambles. The living room stood almost by itself, a shell, with water beginning to drip down through the ceiling.

Craig made one final trip into the room. It was mostly empty now, except for the chairs and the soldering equipment, wires and batteries, on one bench. He began slowly gathering them, thinking in dismay of the costs. Yuri was taking armfuls of file folders from a shelf. "Get the books," he shouted. "The books come next."

An hour later most of the firemen had gone; one remained to watch for sparks, poking around in back.

The three threw themselves on the ground, exhausted. Smoke was wisping through the living room now, water seeping under a far door, and dripping from the ceiling over everything.

"Quick moving job. Thanks," said Yuri. "Glad you came."

"Did we get most of the stuff out?"

"The most important. And my ham tower's safe." He glanced up at the latticed structure above them. "The goddamned bastards." He was disheveled and grimy, but so were they, Craig realized. Damp as well.

"You think it was arson?" Craig asked.

Yuri glanced at him. "I know fucking well it was," he said. "It was tried once before, but I foiled them. They should have known to start in front where my stuff was. The idiots lighted it in back."

Suddenly Yuri grinned, his face—as on the night after the lecture—taking on the look of a satyr. Then the smile faded, and his face was again knotted in fury.

"It's too near civilization here." He paused. "I'm going to have to move to the wilds. Thanks for helping."

"Is there anything we can do?" Lex asked.

"There's plenty to do." His voice was strained with anger. "But you don't know how. I've got to get all my stuff back in sync . . . and . . . No, I'm going to have to move to the wilds. It's too near what's still called civilization here." He looked around. "Lord, what a job."

"Do you have any idea who did it?"

"You're damned right, I know who. I know exactly who. They wanted me to make crank for them. Figured I had the equipment to make it—and the know–how. They were right on that, but I'm not going to hurry the end of this farce.

"I not only told them no, double–damned no, but said if they did find somebody to make it, I'd wreck their set–up. They knew I could do that too. I could get even with them, could stop them in their tracks.

"But I think instead I'll just get out of their way. If I stopped them there'd be others. Crank is home–made and it's vicious. Doesn't take too much equipment, and it makes money by the barrel. It hits the brain, and you don't recover. If there'd been crank in Hitler's time I'd have sworn he and his gang were on it. It makes viciousness seem like fun. It's the latest deal in drugs. Smells like hell when you make it, which is the only clue the police have."

"You could at least call the police," Craig began.

"Me? Call the <u>Law</u>? Give them a hey–day beating up on anybody and everybody just in case? Shit, no."

There was a pause. Then "We're on our way to the wilds," Lex said. "Up in the Smokies. When you find out where you'll be, will you let us know?"

A police car appeared at the bottom of the drive, coming towards them. Yuri looked at it in disgust.

"Well," he said, "here comes the Man."

"Will you tell them?"

"I'll tell 'em it was probably bad wiring. Or my cookstove gone haywire. Naw. You don't call in the Law."

Yuri got slowly to his feet, watching the police car stop, the man get out. He pulled a note book and pen from his jeans, handed them to Lex.

"Put your address and phone down," he said. "Maybe I'll call you. You better shove off now. Might say the wrong thing."

INTERLUDE

The Chinese dragon had slept for centuries.

An ancient civilization, it still retained the electronic symbols of the days of its pre-history, before the world of the west was incubated: Devil doors to protect from nuclear radiation; the yin/yang symbol, precise definition of the structure of the electron. These things remained merely as symbols, their origins lost in antiquity, their true significance long forgotten.

Now new electronics were stabbing its vitals, and its own people were responding with what seemed almost racial memories and tradition . . . the orders of Taoist monks, which had never lost their familiarity with the dielectromagnetic counter-world; the teachings of the Books of Tao, rife with those knowledges when properly translated and understood; even the traditional morning exercises the people went through almost daily spoke with haunting familiarity of the tracing of the relationships in the world of the patterning sequences, the DEM time world.

The dragon stirred and opened its eyes, ravenous. Russia, her ancient enemy to the north, was weakened to near impotence by the revolts of the peoples that had made up her former great estate. China was free to act.

Its first action was to gorge itself on 20,000 of its finest children in a feast called Tiananmen Square.

After the feast it yawned and contemptuously returned to the deception of the Big Lie. There had been no feast.

The lie was successful, first among its own sprawling peoples, then after a bit among the nations of the west.

It opened wide its doors to the businessmen of the industrialized world, who began flocking in to share in the huge market and cheap labor the dragon's peoples represented. The businessmen were met with bowing and scraping, with the formalities of the past; with obsequious attention to their slightest need.

The foreigners dropped their foreign currencies in gushing torrents, vowing to "open the ways between great peoples . . . .

China's most important invited guests—wined and dined and given access to admire its treasures—were the writers and journalists, mostly from the Third World nations, the nations of color.

70

The writers were to tell the stories of the ancient civilizations of their own peoples . . . the stories of all the peoples of color—the Burmese, the Arabs, the peoples of India, the Blacks of Africa, the Mongols of East Russia, the Moslems, the Hindus, the peoples of Brazil, Peru, Mexico, South and Central America, Argentina. "These are the stories that have never been told. This is the market for your talents . . . ."

The stories and books and newspaper articles—even songs— flooded out, marketed by the Chinese to the Third World. The people of the industrialized nations barely noticed.

But the Dragon's peoples were still fractious . . . getting too lively for her comfort.

When a people get jumpy, you turn their attention outward. Let them conquer a few neighbors.

So the second Big Lie was like unto the first. China would solve the problem of the Boat People. Benevolently. After all, she was a benevolent Dragon.

So, benevolently, it swarmed through its neighbor's lands—Vietnam, Cambodia, Thailand.

The armies of China had new allies of which they, as a physical force, were unaware: the burgeoning expertise of the few who took to the new electronics, the DEM frequencies, as to an ancient skill, was clearing their way with invisible broadcasts that created fear, grief and guilt in those people on whom it impinged. It was known to the few who knew as the "Woodpecker Syndrome." Its first use, inexpertly, had been by the Russians, almost a decade past, against their avowed enemies then, the Americans.

The Chinese had not been long in finding and putting to use this new weapon.

The broadcasts took effect long before the armies reached their now almost helpless foe.

The armies of China happily marched in and set about "revitalizing" (the word "subduing" was never used) the countries around and about, unconscious of the fact that their way had been cleared.

It was a training field of no mean proportions.

The nations of the west were aghast. The power structure of their civilization was turning upside down, almost without warning. They were faced with an unprecedented and baffling upheaval in the basic patterns of their antagonisms, with the expressed factor of the final retaliation if they interfered.

China had the bomb. Had had it since the mid sixties, as they knew. And she had delivery systems. She would use the bomb.

Representations were made in the strongest diplomatic terms, but the choice was between words and war. War over Cambodia, Thailand, Burma? Vietnam?

They found themselves impotent against the final threat of nuclear winter. They chose words.

The great dragon that is China had come awake, and was threshing its monstrous tail.

7

When they turned into the long cove that led to their son's drive, the world seemed totally different. Pocked gravel, it was strewn with branches. One larger tree had been sawn apart and pulled aside. Hairpin curves made weaving through smaller branches a hazard.

There was a cloud of dust following them, but the quiet was intense, and the thinner air gave a buoyant feeling.

They turned into the drive leading up the side of the mountain to Jeff's house, peering down into the woods on one side, up into a sky above the ridge beside them on the other. So blue it was, as a Maxfield Parrish painting.

"Oh Craig," Lex said softly. "I feel . . . new."

There was a pasture now, four horses grazing. A medium sized barn, then a log home, with a spread of gravel beside it where a pickup stood; and beyond that the big deck of the house.

Two huge shepherds began barking wildly. The door to the house was flung open and a four year old girl, a six year old boy tumbled out, shouting.

The two youngsters flung themselves on the newcomers with bear hugs and abandon. The two dogs capered wildly at their heels, shoving noses into the melee to be petted, pushing between the four for recognition. Lex and Craig squatted on their heels, hugging and petting, nearly knocked over in the excitement.

Jeff appeared on the outside of the group, and Craig grinned up at him, then slowly rose spilling children and dogs.

Jeff was a younger version of his father; a bit leaner, his face somewhat more ascetic, but with the even, purposeful manner, the relaxed shoulders, that characterized them each. The two hugged, then drew back and looked each other over, each satisfied with what he saw.

Terry came out, wiping her hands on a dishtowel. Slender, almost skinny, with the rangy look of a horsewoman. She flung herself on her father–in–law, then reached down between the children and dogs to kiss Lex.

All four of them were dressed in jeans and boots, with open–necked shirts and wide open expressions of delight.

Young Sean, six, known as Shamus, was a tow-head complete with almost white eyebrows and the skin to go with them. He looked like a Tom Sawyer, and the comparison was inevitable.

Julie, four, on the other hand, had dark brown hair to go with dancing green-brown eyes, freckles, and an expression that seemed to delight in whatever she saw.

Lex had a youngster by each hand as they made their way into the house—a happy mess over an organized base. Books and toys and sewing and half-full glasses of various juices were everywhere.

Terry looked at the mess ruefully. "We are not the neatest," she said, then laughed. Lex joined in her laughter.

"It's ordered underneath," Lex said, freeing herself from the children. "Too neat is too restrictive."

They hugged. The two in-laws got along famously.

Lex wandered over to a big chair, took Julie on her lap. Shamus made himself comfortable on the arm of the chair, his arm around his grandmother's shoulders. She sighed happily, then looked over the children to Terry.

"We'll be staying at a motel in town," she said firmly. "We'll be here for supper, if you like, but we are not going to impose. We're planning to be around for a while. Maybe we'll rent something in town."

"You are not staying at a motel." Terry's voice was adamant. Then she continued, shushing the children as they started to interrupt.

"For one thing we want you here—forever if you will. And for another, didn't you know that motels are dangerous these days? They have guards, but people get robbed and their cars stolen."

"Even here? But that's a small town!" Lex's expression was startled.

"I know. It seems ghastly. But lately things have begun to change. We hoped you were coming, when we heard what was happening in New York. And we hope you won't go back to that rat-race. It may be getting cruddy even in small towns, but it's better than anything that's happening in the cities."

Craig, who had been listening, felt his stomach tighten. He had thought of the mountains—the isolation of the mountains with their tiny towns and their sturdy hill folk—as a safe haven.

74

A place to wait things out. A place where you could stand back and watch as civilization tore itself to pieces and then settled back to a new norm; where they could sit out the inevitable shocks of terror as the sweeping violence of change achieved a more livable pattern.

He looked out the window to where the valley below swept towards further mountains, and his throat constricted as he felt the quiet menaced.

Shamus was pulling at his sleeve, and he looked down at the tow- head affectionately, his mind on the future.

"My name—Shamus—means detective," the child was telling him. "I'm a detective. I told Mom and Dad that you were on your way now. You weren't going to wait. You'd be here. As soon as you could get out of the meg . . . mega . . . out of the cities. Cities," he announced, "are for the birds."

"I did too," chirped Julie happily. "I felt you coming."

Craig turned to his son. "I'll have a bourbon and water. Sour mash bourbon, I hope. With," he sighed, remembering, "good, clean mountain water. If you're out of bourbon, we've got some in the car. I expect Lex will duplicate my order. It was rough getting here. We've stories to tell and things to do."

"You raised me to believe that bourbon and branch—sour mash bourbon and branch—was the only civilized drink," said Jeff. "I'm never out—except when poverty overtakes us between books."

The sun had dropped behind the mountains. Sunset spread blues and golds and grays across the western ridge. The four adults settled themselves on the deck, drinks in hand, relaxing in the clean, cool air, in the quiet, in the distances before them.

The children were galloping towards the meadow, the dogs barking at their heels. Lex had hitched herself onto the deck railing, leaning back against a post. Craig and Jeff and Terry were comfortably side by side in chairs, Craig with his foot canted up onto a child's bench, the smoke of his cigar curling about his head.

"I think space is the ultimate luxury," Craig said softly.

His son smiled. "I see those pictures on TV of New York—or Chicago or Washington or Los Angeles—lit up like all get-out, that are supposed to be so beautiful. To me, they're ugly. Each light represents a cubbyhole with a human or so in it; each one a tiny, spaceless prison, and all I can feel is that I'm sorry for them."

75

Terry laughed. She had been brought up on a Kentucky horse farm; had grown up with space.

"I had a beau once," she said, "when I was young and handsome. A millionaire type . . ."

"You should have married him and lived in luxury ever after," Jeff interrupted.

"That I should have. He wanted me to," she said mildly. "At any rate, he was going to New York to stay in the Waldorf Towers. I felt sorry for him, having to stay in one of those cubbyholes. He asked me, in a twitching sort of way, how I had the audacity to feel that way . . . and I never saw him again. So that's why I didn't marry a millionaire and live in a cubbyhole in luxury."

"You get addicted," Craig said. "Like any caged animal gets addicted. To the hand that feeds you; to the petting and the recognition and being singled out from among the crowds.

"It's quite a real addiction," he added. "It's being washed and combed and petted." He stood up and leaned on the railing, looking out over the cove. "It's being in the bright lights and the quote center of things unquote.

"It's grim and vicious if you look down, but if you look up, if all you let yourself see is the hallucinations—I think it's probably like cocaine. The restaurants where you're greeted by name. The coziness of your own tiny cubbyhole. The importance of the people who beg for your services. The glitter.

"And the lack of time," he added. He was speaking almost to himself, now, though enough to include them as well. "They say that when space contracts, time expands. But it's only that time speeds up, and there are no minutes left. It's a blur of no minutes, no seconds. Only a day or a week that has come and gone before you notice."

When they went to bed that night, in the big comfortable bed of the guest room, the stars so bright in the velvet darkness, the air so quiet, he held Lux in his arms.

"How is your addiction?" he whispered. "Should we stay for a bit?"

She snuggled closer. "I . . . I feel as though I never want to see a crowd again. At least, not until things are under control. Let's not go back until we're sure the lights are on . . . to stay. Until the water is running and the people are laughing and it's fun to be alive."

"It might take months."

She nodded, her head against his shoulder. "Even so. Why don't we rent a cabin somewhere here and wait it out? A couple of months? Or several. I'll get started on my book. You can . . . but what on earth is there for you to do out here?"

He laughed. "I'd find something. I could sketch out the engineering problems of . . . well, of rebuilding. Of the new attitudes we have to take to get sound again. Of what must be done and quickly. Somebody's got to come up with a basic plan. I could . . . take a look at the engineering problems, the way you do for any engineering proposal. At least outline the parameters."

He held her close, thinking casually of the vast network of problems entailed, in the rebuilding of the structure of even one city, until he felt her stretch her naked body sinuously against him; felt her roll on top of him and tuck his burgeoning lance between the warm lips that parted her pubic hair; felt her slow breaths on his neck and the quiet motions as she began the eternal movements of making love.

The uniting held the richness of years, the rewarding knowledges of each for the other, as each explored the protected spots increasing excitement that grew into a violence of sharing and burst into flame.

INTERLUDE

New York was under martial law. It had water, in water hours, sequential over the city; and not much pressure even then.

Back–up generators for power were at a premium, and manu–facturers were working three shifts to supply them. In the tall build–ings water was pumped and usually reached the top.

There was electricity, but it was a brown–out, disastrous for air conditioners, inadequate for heating and cooking. Power sufficient for elevators was turned on twice a day, at nine a.m. and at five p.m. for one hour. Business was done by telephone and fax.

The Stock Exchange had acquired generators, and carried on as though it were business as usual; but the heads of the Securities and Exchange Commission were making plans for building in Virginia. It would be an automated exchange, and they regretfully admitted that the chaos that had characterized the Exchange floor since its inception—and that had been partially at fault for the October '87 crash—would be replaced by an orderly quiet. That chaos had been a way of life for the buying and selling of stocks, and it would be missed, but the new technologies would no longer tolerate the turbulence, and it would vanish like the dinosaurs.

With computers and satellite communications it wouldn't be necessary for the big brokerage houses to move. They probably would, and Trinity Church would live on at the head of a dead–end street.

While they were about it, the SEC arranged quietly to create a Globex link, similar to that set up for the New York Mercantile Exchange, which would give the world a twenty–four hour a day electronic system for trading in all Exchanges. Reuters was in on that, as it had been on the Mercantile Globex, and the exchanges of the world were expected to join in.

The subway systems ran, and trains in and out of the city, but the vast mobs that inhabited them were dwindling. Added now to subway crime was the fear of being caught below ground. Yet to get from one part of the city to another, a subway remained a necessity.

Taxis increased, and did a land–office business.

It wasn't just New York. Across the nation and the world tensions were increasing, and the violent crime that abetted those tensions.

Computer viruses became as virulent in the technological world as the AIDS virus was in the physical—and as unamenable to research for cures.

Computer worms had first become a media spectacular when one of the first cost the Bank of New York five million. The Bank termed it a computer "glitch" or simple error, in an attempt to cover up the threat before its customers panicked.

When a worm caused the USA's MI money supply to bulge to almost twice its ordered size one week, there was quiet terror among those in the know.

A Top Secret label was put on computer crime in the name of National Security.

Los Angeles was the first to form a special police computer crime unit. It proved its worth in its first few weeks of operation. It isolated the subversive coding of a worm in the city's Department of Water and Power just before that Department's one point two million customers were cut off from both water and electricity.

A law was put on the books making computer invasion a federal crime with dire penalties. Research to stop the invasions became intense : on the one side to stop the invasions; on the other to break the defense barriers.

Wild swings in the weather became the norm. Hurricanes re-placed drought. All time records for cold and heat were broken regularly. Barometric pressures went off one end of the scale, and then the other, in rapid changes.

Violent earthquakes were accompanied by mud slides, as the ground responded as though it were fluid.

Then came the flu. The New Flu it was called, more contagious than any that had yet been seen, decimating whole areas until fear stalked the country.

. . . And always the winds . . .

8

Breakfast the next morning was a hubbub of voices and laughter. After it was cleared away, Shamus, Julie and Terry commandeered Lex to go see the horses and the garden.

Craig and Jeff pleaded off and took cups of coffee out to the deck.

"Is our being here interrupting your writing?" Craig asked.

"I'm taking a vacation while you're here. Haven't taken one in a year. I generally get to my typewriter before the chaos begins. I have a small den back behind the kitchen where I can ignore the rest of the world."

"How's it going?"

"The latest whodunit is about half-way through. They're popular enough to keep the mortgage paid and keep us fed. I like writing them. It's rather like putting a jigsaw puzzle together, but it's demanding. If I leave off writing for a day or two, the characters get bored and go off to do their own thing. I have the devil of a time pulling them back into the pattern. They're obstreperous creatures, with minds of their own. Quite often they give me good ideas."

Craig was proud of his son, of his ability and his independence. His face showed it.

"You're well organized, I gather."

Jeff smiled. "Writing is like any other job. You go to the office every day and put in the work necessary—or," he laughed, "you get fired. That is, you don't get the story told in a reasonable fashion and it doesn't sell.

"It is like a job," he added lazily. "If you don't work at it it doesn't work. I'm enjoying this vacation."

Craig took a deep breath of the clear air, put his cup on the deck bannister for a minute while he stretched, then picked it up and led the way onto the field in front of the house. There was an area of level ground before the mountain dropped off precipitously, and just below, a deck built among the trees. He looked around. It seemed as though he could see forever.

Suddenly the quiet was shattered by the sound of a chain saw whirring into life. A second followed, and a third. Then a piece of heavy equipment roared into life.

Craig, startled, looked at his son.

"They're timbering on the next hill over." Jeff's voice held disgust. "It was bought by a newcomer last month, and they're clear-cutting. There's nothing I can do about it. I tried. But the timber will almost entirely pay for the land. The owner was barely civil when I tried to talk to him."

Craig thought of the sixteen thousand trees it took to put out one issue of one major weekly magazine, and he shuddered. It wasn't just in Brazil or the Sudan. It was coming to what he had considered a protected area. How many magazines did he read a week? How much paper did he, himself, use?

He looked around. The trees on these hills were second or third growth already—their roots not nearly so deep as those of the giants that had once covered the continent.

He shook his head. Then: "Your mother and I have decided to rent a place up here. Near you, if possible. For a month or so. Until things in New York stabilize."

Jeff grinned. "You can stay with us—forever if you like."

"No. We want our own place. Do you know of any near here?"

"I wish the one up the mountain a-piece was for rent. It's big and comfortable and you'd love it. But it's just for sale. Maybe . . ." He paused a minute. "I could ask the agent to find out if they'd rent."

"How on earth did you find this place?"

"Walked the hills with the dogs. Just roamed the hills. When I saw this place, I knew it was mine. That's when I phoned you asking for help on the down and the points. Thank you again. Shamus was a year old, Julie was on the way. I wanted to get my family out in the country." Jeff patted his father's shoulder. "I should be able to start paying you back in another year."

"Don't worry about it. When you can."

They stood quietly a minute, Craig trying not to listen to the chattering of the chain saws, to the roar of the heavy equipment that seemed to reach into his innermost being.

"Even with the noise, and the . . . invasion of the clear- cut, the area feels good."

Jeff smiled grimly. "I've thought of trying to move further back, but as far as I can tell, there's no real further back. We're just about up against the far wall."

Craig looked at his son strangely. "You may be right. I hadn't thought of the way things are that way. I guess a lot of my concepts are changing." Then: "Let's go to town. I need to transfer funds here if we're going to stay a while. And we need to talk to your real estate agent about renting."

They took Jeff's pickup.

The bank had a Southern Comfort look—brick with a white portico, chandeliers and curtained windows.

In a corner of the lobby a plump, gray–haired woman was huddled, pulled into herself as though to protect herself from the world.

"That's Mrs. Richardson," Jeff said, "and something's wrong. She's a happy little person . . . ."

She looked up as they came to her, and tried to rise, but collapsed.

"Oh, Jeff," she said, "you heard what happened?"

He sat on his heels at her feet, taking her two hands into his own. "Not yet, Lottie. What is it?"

"We were leaving tomorrow to go to our little house in Florida." Tears began coursing down her cheeks.

"We came down to town to put a change of address in the Post Office, and oh, a few other things. Then we went back and found . . . ."

She stopped a minute until her voice could clear. "There was a big van at the house, and four men loading all our things into it. We had a chain across the drive, and they must have thought we were gone and they'd be safe. Most of the other people up there have already gone for the winter."

Craig stood nearby, anger rising in his throat.

"Tom," she said, choking again, "Tom tried to stop them and—they knocked him down. They even kicked him. He won't go to a doctor, says he hasn't time. He's in there arranging for money and stopping our credit cards and any checks they may write. They took his wallet."

She looked at Jeff fearfully. He gripped her hands tighter. "I tried to go to Tom, but they made me open the hood of the car and they pulled out wire and told me to stay in the car—and there was Tom lying in the grass.

82

"Then . . . then they took a can of gasoline out of their van, and they poured it all over the house and lit it. And I had to sit there and watch our house burn. Tom got up and limped over to me, and we just sat there, holding on to each other.

"Then," the sobs were almost choking her, "we had to walk almost all the way down before we found a house where there were still people. Tom phoned the Sheriff and he sent a car . . . and . . . and . . . ."

Her chin came up, and her eyes became fierce. "We're going home to Florida and we'll never . . . ever . . . ever come here again."

When Tom came out, Jeff went to him quickly. "Do you have a car?" he asked. "Can I . . . .

The man barely heard him. "Rental," he muttered. He brushed past, took his wife by her arm and led her to the door. His face looked dead.

A few minutes later, Craig was invited into the vice president's office, took a seat.

"Rough going," the man said. "I don't know what's happening. We've been such a quiet, sort of retirement summer town. But recently . . . " Then he shook his head. "At least they have a home in Florida to go to."

"I don't imagine they'll find things much better there." Craig's voice was rough with emotion. He hoped he was wrong, but he knew now, definitely, that he wasn't.

He turned to the bank officer. "I need to transfer some rather substantial funds to your bank," he said. "I'm planning to be here for a while." He brought out identification and his bank card. "You may phone them . . . ."

The man looked at the card. "I can't phone that bank," he said. "It's closed . . . their computers are down . . . for the duration. The duration of the crisis in New York, that is. Do you know what's been happening in New York?"

"One of their out–of–town branches could handle most of it."

The banker looked at him quizzically. "Well, I hoped I would-n't have to mention this, but . . . did you know that the govern-ment's been auditing them? They found some major irregularities, and when New York itself closed down, they went ahead. They've stepped in and taken over."

Craig leaned forward from his chair. "You can't transfer funds
. . . ."

"Not for a day or two at least. Yours funds are probably safe
enough, though I've no way of knowing. Meantime, perhaps I
could make you a small loan on your son's signature? To tide you
over . . . ."

"I could use my own credit card for that." Craig found his
whole basis of thinking turning, almost upside down. The parameters of his life were taking on new forms. The problems he had
been watching that had seemed almost peripheral to a basically
solid civilization were suddenly in his lap.

And each problem would have to be solved on an individual
basis. One and one and one. No engineering parameters that he
could draw up would even begin the task of the whole.

I am glad, he thought, that I am not the President, nor the
Governor, nor even the Mayor . . . not even the Mayor of this
small, truly insignificant town.

Just an individual. Just my family. That's what I must consider.

He held out one of his credit cards. "If you will get me the full
amount of cash on this?" he said. "It should take care of my needs
until my bank opens."

When they left the bank, Jeff drove them directly to a sporting
goods store.

"I gather guns are going to be a necessity from here on out,"
he said. Then he pounded the wheel with his fist. "Little Lottie
Richardson! And Tom. Such quiet, sweet people; so bouncy and
happy. Thank God she wasn't there alone when those thugs
came."

"We'd better not leave our families alone on the mountain
after this," said Craig. "When either of us goes to town, the other
should gather the rest of the clan together in the house."

"Terry's good with a gun."

"Nevertheless."

Craig was silent until they were on the road home. When he
spoke, it was in a far—away voice.

"The banking system." He paused. "I have known it was
vulnerable. As vulnerable as the Savings & Loans. The government has been succoring them both for years . . .

"We've paid to bail out the savings and loans. With our taxes. And several of the banks—the bigger ones, at that.

"The government has to succor them, no matter what the cost. That's where and how the resources of the nation are stockpiled and available for use. It's the fundamental fact of a civilization. If they go, the civilization—at least, things as we know them—go too. It's pretty much the living end."

He was silent for a minute. Jeff kept his eyes on the road.

"They're both at hazard to incompetence and greed. They're at hazard these days to the computer–structure of the commercial world, and to the worms that are invading, though those will probably come under control. They're at hazard, too, to Third World loans, which they keep on the books as of full value—like the government keeps social security on the books to cover part of its hazardous deficit.

"The Third World loans are worthless. They could be repudiated at any time. They would have been repudiated years ago if we hadn't kept loaning them money to pay interest and threatened them with reprisal if they didn't accept our austerity rulings.

"They—those Third World countries—hate us. They borrowed to get our standard of living, and didn't get it—weren't structured for it. So they hate us; and they can't exist much longer under the conditions we impose. They'll all get together one of these days and just say `No.'

"I think," he went on, "that I'll be able to get my money out this time. All of it. As your banker friend said, in a few days. There is too much in the way of industrial and commercial financing being held up to let them take longer.

"I think I will take my money out of the market too. Out of everything I've invested in. While the getting is still good.

"Then, I think I want to put that money where I can keep an eye on it."

Jeff laughed. "In a sock? Bury it?"

"No. Do you have a fifteen or a thirty year mortgage?"

If Jeff was startled by the question, he didn't show it. Like his father, he did his thinking and reacting inside until decision time. "Thirty," he said. "The payments would have been too steep for a fifteen."

"How much and at what interest?"

"Eighty–nine thousand at ten percent."

There was a minute's pause. "You'll have paid over three times the original price before you own that house. The interest. You'll have paid around two hundred seventy–nine thousand for that eighty–nine thousand dollar mortgage. Sounds like a good investment to me. I'd like to buy your mortgage."

Jeff stared at his father. Then a big grin broke over his face. "I can pay you our mortgage and pretty soon some on what I borrowed for the down. You wouldn't lose on it."

"We'll see about that part. I think . . . the house you spoke of up the road? Is it solid? A good investment?"

"You'd have to look for yourself. I'd say it was. But—remember the clear–cutting across the way? Remember the guards on the motels? Seventeen miles to the nearest town, and sometimes snowed in in the winter. It's a lovely place, but expensive."

Craig was silent for a long while. Are you sure, he asked himself, that you aren't jumping off the deep end too fast? He hadn't told Jeff everything. He had felt his values turn over, sitting across from the banker in the small town; had been turning the factors of what was happening over in his mind, while Jeff bought guns to protect his family.

"I think we'll be joining you here," he said. "We'll keep the condo for a bit. This is the wrong time to sell it. But I think we'll be staying here."

He knew he had decided; knew that he wanted to set up both families to be independent of the civilization around them.

It would take everything he had. It would leave himself and Lex without an income except for the few residuals from his firm, and the income from her books.

It was a gamble. He could wait and take the gamble, if he took it, slowly. He could wait—but how much time was there left?

If he waited, if he took things slowly, he could put himself in a better position, if he still felt it necessary. Did he have the right to gamble with Lex's life as well as his own?

He knew the answer, even as he asked himself the questions. If he were right, the time was now. The answer was to act, immediately and without reservation.

If he were wrong? There was no way he could hedge on that.

He could hear Kenny Rogers voice singing: <u>Never count your</u> <u>money while you're sitting at the table; there'll be time enough</u> <u>to count it when the dealin's done</u> . . . .

The cards were on the table. It was his call.

The rest of the song played out in his mind. <u>You gotta know</u> <u>when to hold 'em; know when to fold 'em; know when to walk</u> <u>away and know when to run</u> . . . .

It was time to run. He could feel it in his bones.

He turned back to Jeff. "I think you're right about being against the far wall here. I think you're right that there's little further to go to get away. Yes, I've been thinking of the timbering; and of the high winds as well. Winds, tornado strength but not tornadoes. They're not just here. They've been in Seattle, Albuquerque, England, Europe—bowling over tractor- trailers and cars, taking roofs off homes. They're planet–wide. By the way, how do you protect the children from the high winds? They'd bowl little Julie over and roll her down the mountain."

"The winds are quite recent," said Jeff. "We keep the children near the house. The signal is when the horses spook, or the hair on the dogs' necks rises. Animals are sensitive to electrical changes. High winds cause electrical changes that go before them. Or else they're caused by those changes? I don't know. Earthquakes have electrical changes ahead of them too.

"When the horses prick their ears and spook, we all head for the house; and the horses head for the barn. If there's not time, the kids have orders to lie down flat in an open space."

"What about the tree cutters?"

"They head for the cabs of the skidders, or the pickups they drove to work."

"We'll still join you here. We'll go see that house right away."

"They say home buyers normally look at at least forty–five homes before making up their minds?" Jeff's voice was teasing.

"Location is the first criterion." He waited a minute. Then: "I'm scared, Jeff, It's probably what we've just been through. The fairly narrow escape. The thought of all the people who can't escape." He found his hand was shaking.

Jeff stared at his father in amazement. "You really <u>are</u> scared," he said. "More than just what happened in New York, and the bank?"

"Much more. I've realized it's not just New York. Not just the drought. Not just the revolutions that are happening all over the planet. Not just the stupidity that has become a constant of the civilization.

"I keep hoping that Lex is right; that these are the birth pangs of a new and better civilization. That what we see is the fetus separating itself from the structures that have supported it—that will become the afterbirth. I hope she's right, that what I see is a terrifying birth, from the point of view of the fetus; and that we'll have a new world, a new civilization beyond it."

He pulled out a cigar, took his time lighting it. "If that's wrong; if this isn't a birthing, terrifying but vital, then we're just destroying ourselves. A thing in the universe that proved unviable.

"Take just the atmosphere. If we took fifty million cars off the roads tomorrow—there are eight million in Los Angeles alone— we might be able to breathe. If we also replanted the trees, saved the grasses, revitalized the plankton that all produce oxygen . . . trees and grasses and plankton are the earth's lungs, cleaning the air.

"If we shut down the manufacturers—all of them—tomorrow, we might clear up some of the damage. But it can't be done. If, overnight, our banking system were reformed, we might make sense. But it can't be done.

"If we magically got rid of all the radioactive waste that's stored; and all the atomic plants were rebuilt and repaired on more efficient grounds, the strontium ninety already in the testicles of every male on earth would continue to concentrate.

"We're overpopulated. We've eaten the resources of the planet, and our wastes are in such abundance that we're drowning in them. The planet itself can't take much more.

"And all over the world the peoples are restless in a way that's new. Some of it has had good results, some bad; But it's like a yeast fermenting. There's not enough food for the billions, a fact that is beginning to show.

"Not just New York," he said. "That catastrophe was just one of the first rumblings of an avalanche. All we can do is put up a snow fence. If you look you can see the avalanche coming. We haven't got twenty years. We haven't got ten. We may not have any.

"There's a new wind a–blowing," Craig quoted the old Bob Dylan song. "And the world she is a–changing." Then, fiercely, "And the changes seem to be coming at jet speeds.

"Just last week I was living in what I considered a normal world, a sort of fixed world. It wasn't, but I hadn't noticed. Then, when things kicked us in the butt like a mule, Lex and I came to the mountains where things would be safe and sane . . . ."

He drew on his cigar. "Don't say anything to Lex. We'll tell them all what's happened, let them make up their own minds."

INTERLUDE

Ninety–three million miles away, the variety of cycles within the sun were beginning to come together in what bid fair to be one of the most vicious of her normal eleven to thirteen year peaks.

Gigantic flares reached above the sun's surface, spilling roiling protons and electrons in unprecedented volumes into the solar wind, to sweep past and through her planets like tidal waves, replacing the gentler waves that were normal to her patterns. The magnetic envelope in which Earth rested, already pierced by electronic arrows from her surface, was swept closer to her body on the one side by the increasing violence of that solar wind, was streamed away from her on the other.

The altered magnetic envelope created new areas of molten flux within her crust, which began exploding to her surface in volcanic eruptions.

A new volcano rose nearly to the surface of the sea in the Atlantic, sending out tidal waves that lashed at the coasts they encountered.

Around the Ring of Fire in the Pacific, old volcanoes came to life adding their sum of gases to the pollution of her atmosphere.

Sunsets across the planet became magnificent with vivid colors as the rays of the sun slanted through the denser air as she set.

Earthquakes became stronger daily. Tremendous mudslides that accompanied them from the stripped surface buried whole areas . . . .

9

By the next afternoon they had an appointment to see what the children dubbed the "Uppahill House."

Craig and Lex would drive up. Jeff, Terry and the children would follow on horseback, Julie in front of her mother on Maggie, Terry's mare; Shamus on his own pony, Silver.

Watching them saddle and bridle the horses, Craig felt a pang of jealousy. Years since he'd been on a horse, but he could feel the stirrings within him.

It would be a different life here, if Lex agreed. He'd talk to her after they'd seen the house. He'd told her what had happened in town, but not the conclusions he'd reached. She'd have to come to her own conclusions on so drastic a change as he anticipated.

If they stayed, he too could be a–horseback. The fact pleased him.

Down the mountain they went, then up the cove on a meandering road that turned almost into wagon tracks where State maintenance ended.

There was an old log cabin, seeming to have grown into the land, refurbished recently and with a gaily painted porch swing. There was a green meadow, and against the mountain a large modern log home with huge windows and a surrounding deck. A garage in back was built into the mountain itself.

Craig caught his breath. The sky above the mountain top was a deep blue, outlining the horseshoe ridge which put its arms protectively around the valley.

They went up a long drive, then down to a graveled area where sat a car and a real estate agent. She was a large woman with long gold ear rings, blonded hair, tightly trousered legs above high heels.

The heels seemed to Craig vastly inappropriate, here in the mountains, but the woman managed the gravel well. Lex in her jeans and walking shoes looked to be the native; the other the city–come–to–the–country.

They were ushered across the deck, and Craig left the agent bubbling at Lex while he stopped to look out over the meadow, down and down, to where the cove passed from sight between ridge- shoulders, in a V through which the thruway was just visible, and beyond to another range of mountains in the distance.

Behind him were windows stretching from deck level to above his head, wide as they were tall, a single sheet of glass. He looked to be sure, but they were thermopane.

Lose heat, but worth it, he told himself.

Beside him were huge trees that seemed to nest the house in green.

Before he went in, he looked underneath. Built on a slab. I'd be happier with a three-foot crawl-space, he thought, but the timbers were large, and it looked sturdily built.

He went through atrium doors into a great room, cathedral ceilinged. A free-standing fireplace was towards one side carelessly dividing the room without interrupting it, into living area, kitchen and dining.

The walls of the great room were the inside of the logs of which the house was built, cut and scored to make them flat. There was a redwood staircase to a loft, large and comfortable, with a half bath. The interior walls were oak, maple and butternut. There were three bedrooms downstairs, two baths.

Lex walked over to him, took his arm. "I waited until we saw the place," she said. "Do you like it?"

"This place is ours. It's what we've wanted."

"We're talking about renting." Her voice was cautious. "But—I've been thinking. About what happened in town, and what happened in New York, and . . . Craig, could we buy this instead of renting? We could sell the condo . . .

"I don't want to go back, my love. Not now, not ever. I was wrong. It seemed sort of glorious before. But it's gray and dirty and grim. You were right, and we escaped—in spite of my backing and filling. Don't let's tempt our luck! Craig . . . can we . . . would you like . . . to buy this place? And live here?"

He smiled down at her. "Yes," he said. "Decidedly yes. But there's more that I'd like too." His face grew serious. He glanced around. The agent had walked off to give them a chance to talk. He hadn't mentioned renting to her; just that he wanted to see the place.

"The financial structure is at hazard too, as well as the town. I'd like to get all our money out and invest in—well, I'd like to buy Jeff's mortgage; and set up our two places to be independent of the world. But it will take everything we've got . . . ."

She looked at him, her eyes radiant with pleasure. "Oh, Craig ... yes. Yes, yes, yes," she said.

Through the huge windows they watched the horses come up the cove; watched them tethered to a rail fence. Julie and Shamus came boiling in to throw themselves into their arms.

"Will you live here for awhile?" Shamus shouted in their ears. "Will you truly live here?"

Craig looked at their faces, then tousled their hair, feeling their warm and open happiness.

"If we can make a deal, we really and truly will. Not just for awhile . . . but from now and from now on."

They hugged the two mightily, who then ran off to explore the loft.

"That part will be theirs," Lex said, already placing their furniture in her mind.

"The big double wormy chestnut desk will fit well between the big front window that looks over the meadow and the atrium door to the deck, our computers on each side," she decided.

Funny, Craig thought, the computers—actually the word processor part, for Lex always come first. Lex used hers more than he did. His writing was technical, after he'd finished copius drawings. It was her wordprocessor that was always clattering away.

"If we can get our things out of New York." he reminded her. "If things calm down up there enough so we can get things out."

"Oh, you'll find a way," she told him gaily. "If you can get our money out, you can get out furniture. But if you can't . . . we'll make do. The couch will face the TV . . . ."

He looked out. Yes, there was a satellite dish out there. The TV would be in the corner between the front window and the big side window.

The agent, he realized, was at his shoulder. "You only get one channel up here without the dish," she was saying. "The owner will leave it here for a small price, much less than a new one would cost you. She's moving into town, now that her husband is dead, and she'll have cable there."

You don't get but one channel without a satellite dish, he thought, and felt relieved. That meant that you were protected a bit from the high frequency electronic noises of the world. He smiled to himself as the agent prattled on.

He was half listening to her, but in his mind he, too, was placing their furnishings. We'll have to put up bookshelves, he thought. Our Gary Milek painting will go beside the couch there, lending its deep yellows to the room. The Ruth Marsh painting will go over the desk; the Julie Tucker there. Otherwise bookshelves.

"The owner got the quartz for the fireplace from this mountain," the agent was saying. "He painted the quartz with a mixture of boiled linseed oil and mineral spirits, so it keeps that fresh-washed color forever."

The mountain was granite and crystalline quartz, he realized. Then: "You don't have to sell this house to us, it was built for us." Lex's face was glowing as she explored.

"I'll put the garden on the side toward the ridge," she was saying to Terry.

"You will not." Terry was smiling. "That's sapperstone and it won't grow anything."

Craig walked over to them. "We'll build you a raised garden," he said, putting his arm around her. "You're sure?"

"From the moment I saw it."

"No forty-five houses to look at before we can decide?"

She laughed, leaning against him . . . "Not even four houses. This one is ours."

"It's isolated?"

"The better to write in. The better to live in. If it takes forever to get into town to shop, it probably won't be much more of a forever than to shop in a city. And . . . who wants to go into a town any more?"

He smiled down at her. "I'm not even going to haggle over the price," he said. "It would take too long."

He turned to the agent. "It will take me three to four weeks to move my money around so we can buy with cash. But I could put up enough of a down payment, the owner will be protected if we could move in right away?"

The agent tried to hide her delight. "I'm sure that would be fine, so long as you sign a hold-harmless agreement so that if there is damage to the house before the closing your insurer will be responsible. Agreed?"

As he nodded, she glanced out the window at the westering sun.

"I have the forms here," she said. "Could we be—a bit quick about drawing them up? I don't like to hurry you, but . . . I'd rather be home before dark."

"Of course," said Craig. "The mountains are a bit tricky . . . ."

"I've driven these mountains day and night since I was old enough to drive," she said wistfully. "It's just . . . things are changing. I . . . lock my doors now. I didn't use to. And I try to get home . . . ."

"Would you like us to see you home?"

"No. I'll be all right. I'll lock the car doors. I'd rather it was still daylight, though. Am I discouraging you about the house?"

"You're making me even more sure that I want it, my dear. Let's draw up the contract and that hold–harmless thing, and I'll give you a check."

Lex was in seventh heaven, and Craig, delighted to see her so happy kept his burgeoning worries to himself.

Once the family was gathered in the "Downahill House" . . . the name was a natural, since the children had already titled the Uppahill house . . . Craig called a conference.

"Terry, you and Lex make coffee and cocoa; and a big bowl of popcorn? Shamus, get cups and saucers on the table. Julie, put napkins around."

"It is going to be a major conference?" Terry asked.

Jeff smiled. "We are going to advise and consent to a new way of life," he said. "We're a Congress. Craig is the President."

Craig lighted a cigar, pleased with the attitude being created. In his mind the decisions were made; and the angers and emotions that had seethed through him for the past twenty–four hours while he looked at the necessities of those decisions, were under control, pushing from behind, not pulling from in front.

Maybe he was forcing answers before they were necessities. Maybe this was too soon. But that decision had been made, and he would no longer question it.

They settled themselves around the dining table. Shamus left hastily to get ashtrays, then slipped back into his chair.

Craig leaned forward over the table. "What this conference is about," he said, "what we need to do, is to make ourselves as independent of the rest of the world as possible."

"What he means," Jeff interpolated, "is that the world seems to be going to hell, and the plan is to cover our ass . . ." he glanced at the children. "The plan is to protect our families, at least until the worst blows over."

"And," Craig continued, "I would like us to do it so quietly that nobody notices. Nobody at all."

There was a long silence. Then Terry said, "I don't understand it. We've never even locked our doors. If people went away, even for a whole winter, they'd just tie a rope or even a string across the drive to let their neighbors know they were gone. If anything went wrong the neighbors would go in and fix things . . . like a busted water pipe. Now—burning houses! Kicking old men! It's a wonder they didn't murder him. And guards in the mall parking lots!"

Craig spoke slowly. "I think maybe crank has invaded, even up here."

"Crank?"

"It's the new made–in–America drug of choice. It's replaced crack and most of the other drugs. It doesn't need to be imported. Any college chemistry student with four or five hundred bucks can make the stuff in a barn, out of almost over–the–counter materials. A `joint' doctored with crank can turn on five or six teenagers. Sold for about ten dollars, the take goes into five figures a week, wholesale.

"Try it once, your brain is altered for life. Not just until you can be rehabed—for life. It upsets the neural linkages of the brain. The effects are paranoia, suspicion, anxiety, tendencies towards inexplicable violence. Disrupted memory. Sporadic amnesia. Violence, not just for money—for fun.

"It duplicates acute schizophrenia."

"My God!"

"It's not but a few month old. Came in from California. It was into New York before we left. I believe it's here, in this small town, in this countryside. That means its spread around the country."

Jeff leaned back, lighting a cigarette. His voice was thoughtful. Even the children were looking thoughtful and shocked.

"So we've got that to add to the ferocious weather," Jeff said. "The worst winds I've ever seen. Temperature that goes up and down thirty or forty degrees in hours at unexpected times . . . ."

Terry chimed in. "That's just been in the last . . . the last weeks, actually. I thought we were going to get a nice, slow warming from the greenhouse effect?"

Jeff grinned at her. "Whoever told you that a drastic change like switching to a planet–wide greenhouse effect would happen quietly had rocks in his head. You don't change an entire planetary weather system overnight or quietly. I just hadn't looked at what was happening."

Craig tipped the ash from his cigar. "There's one factor," he said, "that you may or may not have noticed. You react to it, but you don't realize what you're reacting to. The recent swings in the electromagnetic spectrum.

"As a consulting engineer, I get odd bits of information that don't normally reach the public, who are not particularly interested anyway. The electromagnetic swings in the past year—possibly two years—have been just as violent as the weather swings, and could be the cause. The magnetic field of the planet is at its lowest strength ever."

"The cause of the jitters too?" Terry asked. "I've been blaming that on the freak weather."

Craig turned to the children, listening big–eyed to their elders, and eating popcorn almost absentmindedly. "These are things you need to know too," he said. "That's why we asked you to be part of the conference. But you don't have to worry too much about them. Just keep them in the back of your minds."

"You'll do our worrying for us?" Shamus asked with a twinkle in his eyes.

"You'll behave as though the great world out there were dangerous, but you'll enjoy it anyhow." Craig smiled at the youngsters.

"There's an axiom in ecological and electrical engineering," he said, "that I never paid much attention to before, because the planet is so vast, and it seemed to me that the changes were small in comparison. The axiom says that if you change the ecology of a closed system—and earth is a closed system—nothing much happens until the changes reach three percent. That's the make/break point. When that point is reached, the entire ecology rebalances, overnight, probably in a manner inimical to man.

"The other half of that equation is that if you change the electromagnetic spectrum of the entire planet—again, nothing happens until the make/break point of three percent. Then your rebalancing is immediate." One . . . two . . . three. All fall down."

The table was silent for a full minute. Then Jeff spoke up. "Maybe we best not waste time getting ready. Maybe we've already run out of time?"

It was Shamus who spoke up proudly. "We'll work fast," he said. "We're fast workers. I'm strong." He made a muscle.

"Me, too," said Julie, clenching her small fist and pulling her arm up into the requisite position.

Very carefully, nobody laughed. Jeff reached down and felt her arm. "Good muscle." He nodded his head.

They tackled it as an engineering problem, listing first the things each house would need.

"Our power sources should be propane," Craig decided. "Gasoline deteriorates in about eighteen months, and we have no idea how long this insanity will last. Propane lasts indefinitely. We should each have tanks to hold about one thousand gallons, I'd say. Then each a propane generator."

"We have a two hundred fifty gallon propane tank," Terry said.

"We'll up it to one thousand gallons. Gas ranges for cooking, instant hot water heaters that run on gas."

"We'll need huge freezers, which we should fill as rapidly as possible." That was Terry. "We could keep them cold running the generators about an hour every other day."

"Chain saws and a log splitter each. Those will need gasoline. We can supplement them with cross-cuts and wedges, as well as go-devils."

"We can bury gasoline at a distance from the houses. Use it until it deteriorates."

Shamus had been thinking hard to find a contribution. "We oughta have gates across the driveways. Keep bad people out."

Jeff looked at his son fondly. "You're right," he said. "Gates that will lock. But around here a locked driveway is a signal to the baddies that you're away for some time. So we'll put them there, but we'll leave them open."

"How—to books," said Terry.

"And school books," said Shamus.

"And picture books for the alphabet," chimed in Julie.

Lex had been sitting quietly at the end of the table. Now she spoke. "You're really thinking big," she said fiercely. "You sound as though you expected the crisis to last for years."

"If there is a crisis, it will last for years." Craig's voice was firm. "It may not get much worse than it is now, in which case it will be resolved and life will go on more or less normally. But the symptoms for a major, planet—wide catastrophe are growing at a fantastic rate. I propose that we crawl into our cave, and pull the cave in after us."

Lex's expression was grim. Then she smiled. "Okay," she said. "Maybe we expect the crisis to last for years—maybe it will go away. At any rate, I for one am sure life will never be the same again.

"Wherefore and whereby," she continued, "If we're to be an isolated group, at least for now, let's behave as though we're the nucleus of tomorrow. Let's set goals and values, goals that would make a world we'd like to live in. And find ways to make them work."

My wife, Craig thought in amazement. She hit the nail on the head again.

Terry was the first to speak. "You're right, Lex. We could codify a set of values—beliefs—for ourselves and try them out. The ones we inherited may be right, but the world is in a mess with them. But where do we start?"

Jeff smiled. "Mom has a structure, you can bet your bottom dollar. I'm with you on the need. What's the structure, Mom?"

Lex laughed. "Prophets are not supposed to be tolerated in their own homes," she said. "But, yes. Part of my work has been watching value structures and how they work. We shan't set the goals over night. I suggest we regularly have Sunday breakfast at our house, and an—well, an ethics meeting after.

"For now, it seems to me we want to be happy, trusting, loving people, and we want the same for our society. For that we have to encourage honesty and openness. We have to tolerate mistakes and handle them as learning opportunities. We have to accentu- ate the positive and learn from the negative. The opposite values are learning by force, fear and coercion. What I mean is the use of force, fear and coercion to achieve anything must be avoided. There must be consensus decision making . . . ."

Craig and Jeff were smiling, and Terry turned on them fiercely. "She's right! Don't try to dismiss this! It's central. If we cannot raise children without resorting to these things—to vio- lence, physical and emotional . . . why we'd be training them in those values we most dislike."

The two men were taken aback. "Honey," said Jeff, "people still need leaders, and decision making is mostly required on an instantaneous basis. Occasionally it must be enforced for everyone's good."

Craig interrupted as Lex started to speak. "Don't beat our guns into plowshares, nor our children into goody two-shoes. We don't need a socialistic bureaucracy with everything decided by committee. Our children must be responsible humans and trained to be responsible to and for both themselves and our community. They must be trained in self-defense and the use of weapons, ready to join us in protecting our freedom as individu- als—and taught the need for whatever actions become necessary.

"Freedom always has been the casualty of too much tolerance. Freedom always has and always will demand that you be ready to stand up and fight for what you stand for, what you believe . . . ."

"Well," Lex said. Then: "Our Sunday conferences should be interesting. Prepare your arguments."

"Do you suppose we're survivalists?" Terry asked quietly.

"I don't know," Craig answered. "A survivalist is one who survives. You don't know until after.

"If things really crash, and after a few years you're still alive and kicking; if you have been able to handle whatever problems arose—then you're a survivor.

"Maybe the Mormons will be. They've been building under- ground retreats and storing food for years. Maybe the Swiss will be—or the Swedes. They have built gas-proof underground shel- ters for all their people together, with enough food, water and medicines for six months.

"Maybe it will be the farmer down the way, who's been living close to the soil all his years. It could be the scum of the earth. It

could be the `takers'—the ones who find what they want, wher-
ever it exists, and take it by gun or force.

"Or it could be the ones who see the avalanche coming; who
have the <u>audacity</u> to look at the potential and make such preparations as are possible.

"It could be no one," he said softly. "No one at all. It could be
that the human race is committing suicide.

"Could the world rebuild after a real catastrophe? I don't
know. Japan was knocked to its knees, burned out, wasted, and
rebuilt itself into one of the great powers of the world in a few
short years. We're an enterprising race, we humans.

"But—survivors? Long after the breakdown; long after the
dust has settled and the rebuilding begins, you could know who
the survivors are.

"Not before."

INTERLUDE

Down through the earth's skin ran the poisons of nuclear waste. Deep into her bowels.

The waters of her surface were polluted beyond bearing.

The plankton of her oceans were dying of that pollution—and they were among the largest suppliers of oxygen to her atmosphere.

In her soils, not only nuclear wastes but wastes of all human kind were buried, sores and cancers to disfigure her.

Fires raged across her dried forests, making miles of her surface arid and featureless; leaving heaps of ashes; sucking oxygen from her atmosphere; adding smoke to its pollutants.

10

The Fall became a game called "Independence." "Know—How."

Shamus and Julie were delightedly part of a big conspiracy known as "Self-Reliance."

When the high winds came, or the violent storms, you learned to get into the house fast; or if you couldn't, you found the nearest clear area and lay flat. When you went out on a hot day, you tied a sweater around your waist—in case.

Craig and Lex were moved into their new home; their furniture in place. That gave the children two houses which they dubbed the "Uppahill" and the "Downahill."

Their two "neighbors" had left for the winter— the Armentrouts in the old log cabin in the valley below them, who had refurbished the place to look as it had 125 years before when it was built, though with indoor plumbing and running hot and cold water—and the Phillips, somewhat above them on the mountain, whose small house nestled into the hillside as though it were part of the mountain.

"You're staying year round?" the Armentrouts had asked them in surprise. "Of course, it doesn't get as cold as up north, but it does get cold, and up here on the gravel road, you may have trouble getting in and out."

They were a pleasant, elderly couple, loving the place as a spot where their children and grandchildren could get away from the city; could explore the woods summer times; could get a taste of the old values.

"But you'll be isolated!"

Lex had laughed happily. "We'll be here to watch your lovely old place, to see nothing happens to it," she answered.

"Then," said Mrs. Armentrout seriously, "we'd better give you a key. The greatest danger is that a pipe will freeze and spring a leak. That can be catastrophic. Maybe you'd go down once in a while and make sure?"

The Phillips, younger and ready to go back to their Florida tourist business, had come in to say goodbye. "May we leave a key with you as well?" they had asked. "If there's any problem, you could phone us . . . ."

The "Independence equipment" was arriving at each house regularly. Included were the basic foods: grains and a grinder in nitrogen-sealed buckets; iodized salt; honey and sugar; powdered milk; all stored in the garages. Both garages were heavily insulated.

The two families roamed the woods in search of blackberries and huckleberries for freezing. There were trips to meat packers to get whole sides of beef and pork, butchered and cut up, which they then cut into smaller "portion control" packages for freezing.

Lex and Terry found an organic farmer, and they all went into the fields to pick their own beans and carrots and onions and the variety of foods that there was not time to grow. They made a root cellar for potatoes.

There were trips to the Farmer's Market for bushels of peaches and apples; and the game of sitting around the dining table, peeling and quartering and soaking them in lemon water before freezing.

It was fun. It was adventure. The freezers were filling and that felt good—to child and adult alike.

Craig and Lex had just finished dinner when the phone rang.

"Jim Lord, a friend from town," Jeff's voice said. "Lives just above the country club, next door to a friend of the Sheriff's. Says there was a big motorcycle jamboree over the weekend, and now there are motorcycle gangs out over the countryside. They're high and they're vicious, he says. He says he was told one gang was headed out Riverside Road, our way. There seem to be too many for the Sheriff's deputies to control. Jim's phoning everybody in the coves that he knows. They may not get here, but we'd better be on the lookout. He says he doesn't think the gangs are after things—couldn't carry them on choppers. They're after money."

"I'll be right down with my guns," Craig said. He turned to Lex. "There are gangs out. Terry is bringing the kids up here. I'm going down."

"I'm going with you."

"You're going to stay here. Get your guns. Terry will bring hers. You two have to defend the children. You're our last line of defense, in case we can't hold off any—invaders." He stressed the word.

As he headed down the hill, Craig passed Terry and the children coming up. He pulled to the side, almost into the ditch, to let them past. He waved and kept going.

He had to figure out how to stop the gangs before they knew they were being stopped. They would react to a challenge—and get through. But if they could be discouraged without a challenge . . . .?

When he got near the foot of Jeff's drive, he found that his son had already figured it out. Jeff had a dead tree hooked to the bumper of his pickup, and was pulling it toward a spot where there was a steep ditch with a rise just behind it on one side, a rocky area on the other, just as steep.

Good thinking, decided Craig. The tree will stop them. We can hide in the brush and take it from there.

Stopping a gang was not going to be easy; but—no matter the price, they'd have to be stopped.

The sun was below the horizon and darkness crept up the valley as they worked.

It took long minutes to maneuver the tree into a position that looked as though it had fallen, its branches and roots tangled in the brush on either side of this narrow point of the road. Then there came the job of brushing out the trail so that the tree's position looked natural.

There was no apparent hurry between them, but the smooth motions with which they did the job wasted no time. Each knew the danger, the viciousness of gangs; each knew that whatever else, they must not let the gangs reach the uppahill house.

They backed the car and the pickup up the cove road, out of sight, a final barrier from which they could fight.

They worked together almost without speaking. Finally, "it wouldn't stand close inspection," Jeff said, "but I think it's the best we can do for now."

They hid in heavy brush above the tree–barrier and made themselves as comfortable as possible, shotguns at their sides, a pistol in each belt, out of sight of the road though almost on top of it.

We should separate, Craig thought, to make ourselves appear more of a multiple ambush. But for now they needed the closeness.

An hour passed, then another, before they heard the growl as five cycles roared up, swung before the tree, were stopped and canted onto their stands, their motors gunned over and over in the deep snarls of predatory animals.

One of the riders got off, swaggered to the tree, a chain around his waist clanking with each step.

"Fuckin' winds," he said. He took hold of a branch and tugged.

"Shit, nobody lives up here," another shouted. "There's easier pickin's down Johnson's Den." He was staying on his bike, his helmet giving him the look of a huge insect in the dark.

A drop of sweat was working its way down Craig's nose, but he did not dare move to wipe it off.

"I heeerd . . . ."

"The hell with what you heered. You come move this mother-fucker. I'm not gonna waste my time on empty land. This's where Charley's timbering. There's not even a hen-house around."

The deep, vociferous bellows as the others kept gunning their motors sounded like the magnified chorus of the giant insects they looked to be.

They can't stand silence, Craig thought. They can't stand to remain still. Even for a minute. Even when they're near their prey. They're high, of course.

The clamor of the motors was almost drowning out the mut-terings of the grunting curses; the gunning of those motors a chorus ululating through the woods.

Craig listened, fascinated in spite of the tensions he felt, fascinated by the paucity of expression, the tribal snarls.

This is the beating of the drums as the primitives go on the warpath, he thought. This that I am hearing is the walking drum that keeps the tribe in step . . . .

As though at a signal, the five cycles wheeled together and scratched out. Down the cove. Out of sight.

Jeff, who had held his gun steady, who had crouched without motion, abruptly began to shake. Adrenaline. Thought Craig. He laid his own gun down and pulled himself to his feet by the nearest bush.

Jeff still crouched, his shotgun across his knees. "That was too close," he said. He looked at his father. "We've got to figure a better defense system."

106

Slowly he, too, got to his feet, stretching to get the blood circulating, to get rid of the shakes.

"Go on up to the house and phone the others," Craig said slowly. "They'll be worried. We're going to have to stay here all night. Just the two of us. We can't guard in shifts. Takes at least two down here. If they'd moved that tree, we'd have played hell trying to stop all five . . . though if we'd killed two with our first shots, the others might have spooked."

He looked at his son. "How quickly we go primitive," he said. "I'd have shot to kill. I hoped that you would. We were facing brutalizers; probably killers."

"Never pull a gun until you are ready to shoot to kill," Jeff answered. "Once you've faced a man with a gun, you've forced him to try to kill you. You taught me that early."

He paused. "I didn't think I'd need a gun, ever. I don't hunt. Now I know."

He looked around at the brush and rock in which they'd hidden. "I'll bring sleeping bags and some food," he said. "We'll figure out a better defense while we watch tonight."

The stars wheeled across the heavens. They wrapped sleeping bags around themselves their voices quiet as they discarded plan after plan.

No locking of the stout gates they'd installed across the cove road; that would be a challenge to marauders. A light beam across the road, with wires to the one house? The other could be alerted by telephone. That would at least give them warning, and it could be done . . . .

Jeff took the first watch at well past midnight. When he finally shook Craig awake it was almost daylight.

The morning was bright across the mountains when Craig heard a motor and quietly waked his son.

A green army jeep came down the road, stopped at the tree. The two in the brush stayed hidden, shotguns ready.

A youngster in uniform got out, gangly, with the loose–jointed stance of a mountain man. He called to his partner who had stayed in the jeep.

"Somebody got right smart," he called. "Pulled a tree across the road."

His partner climbed lazily from the jeep; older, a bit stiff, with the beginnings of a pot. "There's wheelies in the road," he said. "I expect the outlaws got here."

Jeff looked at his father, who nodded. He stood up slowly, leaving his gun at his feet in the brush. Craig stayed where he was; invisible.

"Hi," Jeff called to the soldiers. "Yeah. The outlaws got here. A motorcycle gang."

"They stopped at the tree, Sir?"

"Right."

"You're lucky. There've been people murdered in some coves."

"Yep," said Jeff. He wasn't ready to commit himself yet.

"Martial law was declared yesterday. Took a bit of time to get us out." The youngster was grinning. "We're putting National Guard at most of the crossings. We already got the guys who were probably the ones came here. You all right? You alone?"

Craig stood up slowly, his gun in the brush. "We're all right," he said. His voice was tired. "We're sure glad to see you guys."

The youngster looked from one to the other. "You'll be all right now, Pops," he said. "We're patrolling. But mostly we'll be at the intersections where anybody has to go through. You just rest easy, now. The country's under control."

"You'll have to move the tree, though," the older man chimed in. "So we can patrol," he added.

"You don't need to worry," the younger said. "I was born just ten miles down the road. I know this cove like the back of my hand. Used to hunt here." He grinned disarmingly. "There's only this one way in, no other way out. We'll keep you safe."

Nevertheless, Craig thought to himself, we will get that light beam system installed. And anything else we can think of.

It was October before it was realized that the violent hurricanes and typhoons that had swept the coasts of the world were not ending with the season. Nor were the violent winds that swept the interiors of the continents.

Craig, watching the news, realized that the high winds had been almost accepted as part of the scene, and people were simply making provisions of a sort to accommodate them. They themselves had taped their windows, and stacked their firewood on the deck in such a manner as to barricade the bigger windows.

So quickly we adapt to whatever Mother Nature dishes out, he told himself. So quickly we become immune to astonishment, and make our way through turmoil.

As in the wars and revolutions across the planet. Frenzy and horror at first, then attention to the details of living took over. The business of money and food and water—growing scarcer—dropped to—if not acceptance, at least accommodation.

There was a new flu now, that looked to be worse than AIDS. A paralytic flu with sporadic outbreaks that seemed to come from everywhere—England, China, the central countries of Europe and Asia; even in the southern hemisphere.

The symptoms were simple—what seemed to be a head cold that hung on for weeks, then vomiting and cramps; finally a paralysis, not just of the arms and legs, but of the internal muscles as well. Once the paralysis hit, death was almost immediate.

At first it was called the New Flu, a word that changed quickly to the dread word Para.

Hospitals began refusing admittance to anyone with "colds," and a great outcry of discrimination was raised that was quickly smothered as the violence of contagion of Para was recognized. "Hospitals are set up to handle contagious diseases," the National Health Department insisted. The hospitals became adamant, and the argument went to the floor of Congress.

Fear was as contagious as the Para, not only of the disease but of the increased lawlessness it engendered. Neighbor became afraid of neighbor. Even families watched each other closely. Liquor sales became tremendous, the drug scene expanded, as people tried to insulate themselves against what was happening around them.

Craig finally came to realize that fear was as virulent a poison as any other, and one to which they had not given sufficient attention.

From contact with the outside, we can protect ourselves, he thought. Fear comes through secret channels, and only one's innate pride can conquer. You cannot refuse to recognize it; it must be recognized for what it is and battled internally.

He talked to the children on walks to feed the horses. He talked to Lex and Terry and Jeff. Pride, he told them. We need not be ashamed to be afraid. We need only be afraid to let it rule us.

Craig stood on the deck of the downahill house, watching the beginnings of color in the west. The recent resurgence of volcanoes around the Ring of Fire had spread their ash through the upper winds, and sunsets had become spectacular . . . reds and purples and gray–blues, and the great orange globe of the sun setting atop the distant ridge. He took a deep breath—

And held it. It had sounded like a scream, but had shut off so abruptly he wasn't sure. He listened, but there was nothing more.

It could have been . . . could have been . . . .

He reached inside the front door and got the shotgun there. Then, hesitating only a second, he added Terry's small twenty–two pistol, sticking it in his belt, beneath his sweater.

Jeff had gone on one of their few trips to town. The others were at the uppahill. He was there to feed the horses.

The sound had come from where the clear–cutting was ended for the day. Instead of the drive, he headed down a path that led steeply to a creek, forded it, and stepped into the woods on the far side.

The woods were torn from the careless cutting. There were stumps and heaps of branches everywhere. He tried to walk quietly, but it was almost impossible.

Off to his right he heard a high pitched laugh, then a gruff voice: "Outta thuh way. I wanna feel the nice pussy . . . ."

He turned fast in that direction, and felt the shotgun snatched from his arm.

"Hey, this here's prob'ly her daddy. He can watch . . . ." The shotgun was against his ribs. He started to turn, snatch it, found himself shoved by the barrel into a stumble.

It was a bearded face, split by a huge grin; the eyes above the grin brilliant with hate. Insane.

Helplessness swept over him. He was caught. In the hands of berserkers, of crazed druggies.

It was only a few steps to an opening in the brush, as he was prodded by the shotgun. Only a few steps . . . .

110

There were two others. One a grizzled boor around fifty, with greasy hair and a scraggly beard; the other a youngster not more than nineteen. The one behind him he could no longer see.

Stretched on the ground, her arms pegged out wide, was Terry. Her shirt was torn open, a dirty bandana gagged her mouth; her hair was over her eyes; her boots off; her jeans and panties pulled half down.

Fear caught at his throat. The shotgun in his ribs told him that if he made a wrong move, he'd be killed and there would be no succor for Terry.

Her lovely, rangy strength brutalized and ravaged by animals. Her clean intelligence savaged by a wolf pack . . . and she, probably killed.

I should have known the possibility. I should have expected . . . I have been civilized too long. How much more would it have taken to make me see . . . to make me take precautions from . . . this? What do you have to have rubbed in your face before you look, look to really see, the depredations . . . and their nearness . . . the avalanching dementias gone berserk; the insane, like dogs, at your heels?

He felt his gorge rising, and the fear turned to fury. An ancient fury, a rage that burned up from his toes to his brain, nearly blinding him. A roaring of fury in his ears.

With a violence of will that was as physical as it was mental, he forced the rage down and back; down to where it would push from behind, not pull blindly from in front.

If she is to have any chance at all, he knew with a frigid certainty, I must stay sane. Find the chance. Use it—not throw it away.

The gun in his ribs prodded, and he let it push him nearer. The voice behind him was guttering with pleasure. "After we get tired of the front," it was saying, "we'll turn her over Daddy's knees and fuck her in the asshole. It's tighter and it'll bring you on after a long night. Her daddy'll . . . ."

The man's attention was half on what he was saying. Craig pivoted on his heel, smashing the shotgun from his ribs with his arm, feeling the shot tearing his shirt; pulling the twenty-two from his belt and shooting the man behind in the stomach.

In the same pivoting movement, he changed his aim to the grizzled, dirty oldster kneeling beside Terry, and shot., There was

111

no time to aim. The bullet got only the shoulder. He shot again, this time in the chest. The youngster was screaming.

He turned, twisting, to the man behind, doubled over now, and put the pistol to his head, pulled the trigger. It splat as it came out the other side.

The youngster was running, and he let him go. The man behind him was dead. The older man by Terry was swaying.

Craig snatched up the shotgun, grabbing it by the barrel, and swung it against the man's head. The man went down with a groan. Craig raised the shotgun by its barrel again and brought it down with all his strength onto the skull, feeling the skull crack, feeling it crush under his blow.

He stood a minute, making sure. Then he knelt by Terry, his hands shaking as he unpegged her arms, pulled off the gag.

She sagged on the ground, tears pouring from her eyes. He took her in his arms and held her close.

"They're dead?" she asked through her sobs.

"Two of them. The youngest one ran."

"They . . . they . . . ."

"Quiet," he said softly, forcing steadiness into his hands and body. "As soon as you can, we'll get out of here."

"I was . . . I was hunting berries . . . they . . . they . . . ."

It was a long way back to the house, to his car, to getting her into the car. On the way to the uppahill house, she took command of herself, dried her tears; but her shaking didn't stop. Craig forced his own legs to quiet, kept his hands calm on the steering wheel with will power.

Terry was in a hot bath; Craig had a strong drink in his hand; Julie and Shamus were playing outside as they had been when Craig and Terry drove up.

Lex came out from taking care of Terry. "I'll call the Sheriff's office," she said, picking up the phone.

Craig found himself batting the instrument violently from her hands.

"You will _not!_" He realized that he was shouting; tried to quiet his voice; tried to still the shaking that had begun again and that was spilling his drink.

112

She was staring at him.

"You will not—call The Law." He noticed he'd used the colloquial term. He leaned over and picked up the phone from the floor, subconsciously listening to its recorded voice saying "If you want to make a call, please hang up and try again. If . . . ."

"You," his voice was still not quiet. "You—nor any of the others—will tell anyone what happened. Nobody. Nobody at all." His voice grew fierce, shaking, almost shrill.

"Don't you remember? We handle our own problems now. We don't call anybody in to help. We don't depend on anybody." He found he had his hands on her shoulders, almost shaking her. "You understand?"

Lex looked in his eyes, carefully took his hands from her shoulders.

"I don't understand," she said. "Not completely. That was Terry's twenty-two, registered in her name. It killed two men. The other ran . . . ."

Craig shoved his hands in his pockets, turned away from her, then turned back. "Their bodies will be found," he said. He wouldn't be able to make her understand. It would have to be by command, and neither had ever treated the other that way. "We will be questioned. We heard nothing. Know nothing. Julie and Shamus must not know so they can't be tripped up when questioned.

"The bullet cannot be identified without the gun, and we have the gun. If it is found, it was stolen. They only have a few twenty-two bullets. They can't trace it." Maybe she'd learn to understand later?

She looked away, then. "I guess I've got a lot to understand," she said. "I've got a lot to learn about you." She turned to go back to Terry, then turned again at the door. "You've changed," she said. "Sometimes I think I don't really know you at all, any more."

It was only a few minutes later that Jeff drove up. He had a passenger.

"Found the guy at the foot of the cove, asking for the Gallaghers," he shouted to Craig happily.

Craig watched in surprise as Yuri Malchek angled his way out of the pickup.

Yuri. What a time for that astringent young man to arrive.

113

Jeff came up the walk first, and Craig took him by the arm. "Terry and Lex are in the bedroom," he said softly. "Go in there and <u>don't come out until I call</u>."

Jeff was startled, but obeyed instantly, and Craig turned to greet Yuri.

"Hi!" He had his voice under control now. Maybe I'm learning, he thought as he listened to himself. "I didn't expect you way out here."

"You said you were going to the wilds, and I was looking for the wilds. I like what you've found."

The young man's manner hadn't changed. Voice and stance were those of a superior officer addressing a non-com. His hands were in the pockets of his jeans, but his hair was still clean and neat; his jeans pressed; his sneakers L. L. Bean. And his eyes were clear.

They entered the great room, and Yuri looked around, then turned to his host.

"This sure would make a good lab," he said, and grinned.

Craig felt himself calmer now. He looked the young man over, the high cheek bones, the lean, intelligent face, the long slender nose, the muscular arms, the quick stride. And, he thought, that look of a satyr. Gruff to cover a sardonic distaste for the world . . . even as my distaste, he thought. With me, not distaste, a growing terror . . . .

"This house is taken," he heard himself saying. But, he thought, we could use you . . . and your electronics. And, he added to himself, your ham station . . . .

"Have a drink?" he asked. "Bourbon and water available."

"Sure," said the other.

Craig went to the cupboard for a bottle, and was surprised that Yuri headed for the refrigerator and got out ice cubes to drop into the glasses that Craig offered. It was a comfortable action, not pushy; not taking over. Just doing what came naturally, as though he belonged in the house.

Drinks in hand, Craig led the way to the deck. In the meadow below Shamus and Julie were building a structure of the rocks that were lying around. They waved gaily and went on with their game.

Craig leaned on the banister and looked out over the meadow to the V where the cove wandered between two small ridges; to the tall ridge in the far distance. Yuri set his drink on the banister and stretched.

"You sure pick well when you pick your wilds," he said.

Craig looked at him, his decision made. "There's a place up the hill from us," he said. "Not grand, but comfortable. The owners are summer people. They might rent. The Phillips."

"Have to be a long rental. I have to set my stuff up, wire it in. Set up my ham tower . . . ."

"The way things are going, it might be a very long rental. They only come up a couple of weeks a couple of times a summer."

Yuri smiled lazily. "Be worth a chance. You know how to reach them?"

"You haven't seen the place. It's a hoot and a holler up a piece."

Yuri turned to him, his face serious this time, rather than grim. What a difference his expressions make, thought Craig. His face is . . . malleable? No. His expressions come from inside, and alter his entire being, he decided.

"It's the wilds I want. I can make do with any kind of place. Especially," he added, "if I can heat it for the winter. But then, I could put in a stove . . . ."

Craig laughed, and the release from the tensions of the last few hours was so great that the laughter played through his body, refreshing it as the drink had not.

"You know how to get in touch with them?" Yuri was asking. "I have my stuff in a U-Haul trailing my pickup, down the way."

"I have their phone number. They live in Tampa."

It was fairly easy to arrange. Craig told the Phillips he had an old friend whom he'd guarantee, who wanted to rent their place for the winter, and the rest went smoothly. They'd be glad of the extra income from the house which would otherwise be vacant.

INTERLUDE

It was not the starving hordes of Ethiopia or the Sudan or Bangladesh that heard China's clarion call to pride and unity of the Third World. Those hordes had been long since abandoned by their governments in the cities which sequestered donated aid shipments to themselves in order that the hordes be sure to die out. They were, in any case, too debilitated to react.

It was the oppressive governments and the leaders of the guerril-las that opposed them that began to see the white imperialists as their real enemy. They had profited in arms and monies from the white man's largesse with its terrible retribution of debt and regula-tion. Now they would profit from his defeat; would take over his wealth; would have the industries he had built within their borders.

As to the starving minions, they had never counted in any reckoning, and they would not count today. The battle cries that led the able-bodied would change from denouncing internal suppres-sion or the suppression of one religion by another, to castigating the oppressive of the luxury-living imperialists of the white man's smoth-ering demands on their lives and economies.

The activists—the continual fighters of the Palestinians, the Iraqis, the Iranians, the Lebanese, the Central Americans—even the Philippines—the ones to whom warfare had become a way of life—those were well armed by the weapons makers of the world.

The rest—Brazil, Argentina, Mexico, the Mongols of Eastern Russia, the Afghans—they would go along. In some parts of Africa there was a move towards unity rather than the bickering among themselves which left the white man master; but that would take a while.

In the Americas to the South it astounded many to find the large percentage of those of Chinese descent who were among them: business men, industrialists small and large. Given the leadership of China itself and the new pride of color, it took little time for the Chinese among those nations to assume major roles in the leader-ship that was growing to a peak. The nations of color were recogniz-ing themselves as equals—as possibly masters—in the newly a-borning global village.

Off the coast of Africa, morning dawned in a spray of gold between broken clouds over a hill to the east of Bones' ranch-style home tucked in near the beach with its pier, and tied alongside her

116

long range, high–powered speedboat that could cross the Med to Sicily, or Greece or go to Tunisia in a few short hours—and none the wiser.

As with previous mornings since her return, she got up fixed herself a cup a coffee in the micro–wave, and turned her high–powered short wave radio to BBC, London.

It was her daily aphrodisiac—to listen to the news, to hear the latest head–count of the deaths from the new flu, the Para . . . the paralytic invasion that had turned out to be even more terrifying than she had dared hope.

The reports from the capitals of the word were guarded; the deaths undoubtedly underestimated by half. Trying to keep their peoples calm was proving a losing battle, though, as neighbor saw neighbor succumb. Most of Europe seemed to be in the same condition as at the time of the Plague epidemic of the Middle Ages.

All had gone well with her couriers except for one, but that was no problem. He had done his job in the terminal of Singapore, but the plane had a mechanical problem. In terror Simas had tried to get out of the plane and run, and had been shot and killed by a guard.

The epidemic was probably reaching high, now. The news noted that the Prime Minister had abruptly canceled two political appearances, and in the United States, the Congress was having difficulties making a quorum.

The smile on her face made it appear more skeletal than ever.

11

The country lay quiet . . . quiet, that is, except for the maturing violence of storms, the increasing strength of earthquakes, the stories of volcanoes coming alive, the daily toll of Para deaths on the TV.

The word that an earthquake had created a nuclear disaster at the Oconee plant in South Carolina near the North Carolina border upset them; but except for the fear of radiation encircling the earth, it seemed impersonal compared to other disasters . . .

. . . Impersonal, that is, until the light beam, installed now at the foot of the cove, was broken and both houses were alerted to a vehicle coming up the cove. Jeff instantly phoned the uppahill house and kept the wire open until he could report that it was an official vehicle, had come to them, and the all-clear was in order.

As soon as it was gone, Terry phoned. Craig answered. Lex had gone up to Yuri's.

"I've got two babies." There was distress in Terry's voice. "He's on his way to your house with your evacuees . . . ."

"You've got _what_?" Craig was sure he'd misunderstood.

"Evacuees. Babies. They're evacuating everyone from the area of the Oconee plant. My babies—my evacuees—are about six months and about two years old. Their parents were killed. I . . . I . . . you don't have any choice in the matter," she said. "They're dirty . . . and sort of emaciated. They're Mexican, I think. Their parents were working in the fields . . . ."

"We have potassium iodide tablets. They're what you use when you've been exposed to radiation. They absorb and dispose of the radioactive particles. But I don't know how much a baby should get. I'll bring some right down. You don't have any choice about taking the babies?"

"No." Terry's voice was shaking. "The soldier who brought them told me. He just appeared with the two babies and . . . and . . . I guess I can handle it. I've got no diddies. I've got no . . . I'll send Jeff into town right away. He can come by your place and pick up the tablets. I'll bathe them good, scrub their hair, wash their clothes. Even the two year old's shoes. Wrap them in blankets while their clothes dry."

"We'll come down right away and give you a hand," Craig said firmly. "But don't let Jeff go into town. We've got some flannel sheets we can tear up to make diddies. They won't be as convenient as disposable diapers, but this isn't a convenient sort of world any more."

"But . . . they're on their way to your place. This . . ."

Craig looked out the window. A carryall was coming up the road that climbed beside the meadow.

"Okay. It will be a while before we come down. I can see the carryall coming here. Do the best you can—but don't anybody go to town. We'll call you."

Craig was standing in the drive as the carryall drew up, his tall lank figure spraddle–legged; his big shoulders hunched; his hands in his pockets.

A smartly uniformed Sergeant hopped out, blond hair close cropped; a thin mustache on his upper lip.

"Mr. Gallagher? Howdy," he said. "I've brought you . . . ."

The back door of the carryall opened and a lean, scrawny man of about twenty–five climbed out. He had a scraggly beard. He was dirty and unkempt. His eyes, squinting in the bright sunlight, roamed around.

"Purty lonely here," he said to the Sergeant. "How's about you put us somewhere in town? You know, with people around."

"You're lucky to be alive. And these nice folk will take care of you."

"Jimmy," came a nasal voice from within the vehicle, "there's snakes and bears and things in the mountains. I'm sceert. And we almost fell off the edge, getting here."

A younger nasal voice chimed in. "I wanna go home!" it said.

"This is where you're staying," said the Sergeant in a voice of authority. "You can give Mr. Gallagher a hand with the work, and your wife can help with the cooking and cleaning. See that you do."

A female foot in a worn boot appeared, and the woman started to get out.

"I dint tell ya ta get out," said the man fiercely. "You don' get out till I say."

The boot withdrew.

Craig felt his mind go ice cold. He looked at the specimen before him as at a bug.

119

The man squinted at the surroundings again, then back at the carryall. "I don' wanna . . . ."

"You will get out and you will stay. And you will help with the work." The Sergeant shoved the man aside and reached in the vehicle to pull the woman out.

"Okay, okay. You don' need ta get rough. Get out, Emily," the man said roughly. "You, too, Junior. We'll see wha' happens later."

The worn boot reappeared, sockless, followed by a wilted dress under an inadequate sweater, and a face almost hidden under stringy hair. Then a youngster of about ten, as scrawny and unattractive as his parents.

Craig looked at the trio through a film of anger. Were they carrying the flu? Probably not. The difference between the eyes of a druggee and the dying were pronounced.

Was there any way he could refuse to have them in his home? Not now, he decided. There was no use bracing the Sergeant. He had his orders.

"Sorry, Mr. Gallagher," the Sergeant was saying quietly. "The people with any funds can generally find a place to evacuate to for themselves. But these rag–tags and bob– tails . . . well, the law says . . . ."

Craig interrupted the soldier in frigidly formal tones. "I believe you have no authority to make decisions as to where these people are taken?"

The Sergeant drew himself up. "No, Sir. I do not. But I do know they're trying to put as many as possible in the boondocks . . . ." He looked at the gracious house. "Excuse me, Sir. As many as possible in the country to keep from concentrating the problems they represent in the cities and towns."

A huge gust of wind swayed the trees above them, and the three newcomers cowered against the carryall.

Craig waited until the wind had passed, then asked, "How many evacuees are there?" Still in the formal tone.

"Thousands. I don't know how many. But the winds are carrying the fallout east, so they're sending these people west. I . . . ."

"I understand, Sergeant. We will do our best." He turned to the three as the Sergeant drove off. "I am going to take you in and straight to the guest room," he said. "You may be covered in fallout particles. You will shower thoroughly, scrub your hair, and give me your clothes. Including your shoes. I will scrub them thoroughly."

"We gonna be bare–ass naked while you wash 'm?" the man asked.

"We have extra jeans and sweaters." He realized his voice was harsh. These are human beings, he told himself. And probably scared . . . the word came to his mind . . . shitless.

As they entered the house the woman spoke up. "Ah'm a respectable women. I cain't wear no jeans . . . ."

Almost he let his temper flare, then brought it under control.

"Jeans will protect you from the cold," he said quietly. "I'll fix some hot soup for you."

When Lex came in, the three were cleaned and in bathrobes. She looked around in astonishment. They were eating soup and thick bread and coffee—they had refused milk—as though they hadn't eaten in days. Their voices, when he introduced them, were whining.

Wind shook the house, and the boy dived under the table, the woman quailed in her seat. "Them trees gonna come down on us," she said.

"Shaddup," said the man.

Craig pulled Lex into their bedroom for a war conference. At first she was aghast, then pulled herself together.

"It's part of the whole picture," he told her. "This, though, is something I didn't predict."

She looked at him through wide eyes. "But . . . ."

"We knew it would get rough, even up here," he said. He shook his head. "I think I'd rather face wild animals."

She started to throw herself into his arms, but he drew back. "Not until I get cleaned up," he said. "We must not let them make us feel degraded." Then he smiled. "We're able to handle anything that comes along, remember?" Yet he knew that there was no possibility of keeping these people and their community remaining strong.

In one unpredicted instant their lives—their future—had been wrecked. He squared his shoulders, thought of the woods, of accidents that could happen in the woods. Then shook himself. This was not a life or death situation, he told himself.

But he knew that it was.

Could they change these people . . . make them at least a factor they could live with? Breakfast, lunch and dinner. `All day, all night, Mary Ann . . .` he heard the tune hum in his head.

The answer was no, and he knew it. They couldn't have them here, but there had to be a less drastic cure.

"We'll put them in the old log cabin," he said firmly. "Let them fend for themselves as much as possible." At least until I can find a solution, he thought to himself. He couldn't consult Lex on that. It was his job. Where had their closeness and his tolerance gone? Lost, somewhere back in the woods with those maniacs savaging Terry . . . .

"I don't think they could fend. Even partially. I don't think he could even build a fire if you brought the wood in for him." Her voice was low, distressed.

"I'd rather take care of them down there than here," he said. "See if you can find some jeans and warmer clothes. As soon as they're dressed, I'll take them down, and we'll turn on the water and the electricity and build a fire and rustle some food down there."

"The Armentrouts have the place so lovely and clean and homey . . . I hate to do it to them."

"I'd hate worse to do it to us." He kissed her lightly on the forehead. "The Armentrouts are summer people, and they have to take their chances as much as we do. We'll be doing the work. They're just as much subject to evacuees as we are."

Her chin came up. She forced a smile onto her face. "We'll cope," she said. "Maybe—out here—they'll change?"

He smiled down at her, but: "Good girl." was all he said.

It was a strange procession that went down the steep driveway towards the lovely old refurbished log cabin. Lex was doing her best to comfort the woman, who walked in the center of the gravel drive, holding on to Lex's arm in a vice–like grip.

Craig, behind them with the man—Jimmy—and Junior, could hear the whine over the wind noise.

"I cain't," the woman kept saying. "I cain't go up and down mountains. I'm skeert of snakes. And spiders. And thar's probably bears and things. And fallin' down trees . . . ."

The wind gentled for a moment, and Craig could hear his wife's comforting voice. "This cabin," she said, "is one hundred and twenty-five years old. Maybe older. It's stood all that time. It's sound. The owners have put in indoor plumbing and running hot and cold water and electricity and all the things you're used to. You can be very comfortable here."

Lightning sheeted across the high overcast, and the woman tightened her grip on Lex's arm, pulling closer for protection. Craig shuddered.

Once inside the cabin, Jimmy looked around, then turned and followed Craig to the kitchen where he was turning on the electricity.

"It's okay for you, Pops," he said, "to live out in the wilderness. But me and Emily and Junior . . . I don't think we're gonna like it."

Craig ignored him as he turned to the water cut-off.

"Where're we gonna pick up a stash—or a hit—way out in this godforsaken forest? I got caught with only a couple a' days supply, and I get real jittery if I cain't get a stash. You won' like it. You better fine me a answer."

Craig straightened up and looked at the man coldly. "I suppose," he said, "that you mean marijuana when you say `stash'"

"Tha's right. Tokes. A joint."

"And something harder—heroin or cocaine—when you say hit?"

"Yep. An if'n I don' get it . . . ."

"You won't get it."

"I'd better. You won' like . . . ."

"You won't get it."

Jimmy's voice took on a wheedling tone. "You wouldn't have to get it fer me. Prob'ly wouldn' know how. Jus' get me to a city—any city—and leave me alone a coupla hours."

Craig looked at the man as at a bug that should be smashed. His tone was icy. "We will feed you. We will see that you have sufficient clothes. We will make room for you in our lives. We will not make it possible for you to get hold of anything in the way of drugs. We will actively prevent that."

"Square. Damn fuckin' square. You don' know what it's like."

"Nor do I intend to find out, except possibly from watching you."

"How fur t' town?"

"Seventeen miles. Mostly steep. If you leave here, you will not come back."

The man Jimmy subsided.

It took about two hours, getting a fire built in the stove; getting water turned on, the electricity turned on, food in the larder. Basic provisions were already there, but eggs and meats and potatoes and daily provisions were lacking.

During the entire time, Emily huddled in a corner, weeping. Junior refused even the slightest request unless it came as a command from his father. Jimmy watched, made one attempt to be useful, then subsided.

"Wha' do we do if'n there's bears?" Emily wailed the refrain over and over.

Finally, "Shaddup!" Jimmy shouted. "Jus' keep your damn trap shut. I'm a–figurin' things out."

When the cabin was warm, the work done, Craig showed Jimmy how to set the stove to keep the night, then decided to come down at nightfall to set it himself.

"Be careful of the water," he told them. "The cabin is on our spring. We're not on a city water supply and the long showers you took when you got here may have lowered the level in the cistern."

Whether he had made any impression at all, he could not tell.

As they left to go back to their own home, Emily ventured to speak. "Ah won' sleep a wink," she whined. "All them barrs . . . "

"Shaddup," said Jimmy automatically.

The minute they got back to their home, Lex got out soapy water and disinfectants and headed for the guest room and the guest bath.

It was about ten the next morning when Craig heard a hail from below. He went out on the deck. It was a clear day with no wind. A pleasure, except . . . .

"Come n' git me in y'r car," Jimmy shouted. "I cain't walk that hill agin."

Craig hesitated, smothering fury, then shouted, "Okay."

It was just Jimmy this time. He didn't speak until they were parked behind the big house. He made no move to get out.

Then: "Ya don' want us, an we sure as hell don' wanta stay heah."

Craig nodded. "True enough," he said. "But we have no choice."

"I cud give ya a choice."

Craig listened, silent.

"Ah'd need, like, cash. And ya'd have to take me to a city . . . say Chattanooga. I got friends there. Then ya'd be shut of us. We sure wouldn' be a–comin' back to this god–forsaken place."

Craig nodded, refusing to let himself hope. "Might be," he said calmly. "How much cash?"

"Well," Jimmy was almost smiling, a crafty, half–hidden grin. "I figger you wouldn' even miss a thou."

"You mean a thousand dollars?"

"Yup. Tha's what it'd take."

"No way," said Craig.

"We cud trash your place more'n a thou in no time flat," Jimmy told him smugly. "Be a real bargain for ya."

"I'd have the Sheriff here in no time flat," said Craig. He paused a minute, then added. "However, it does seem like a good proposition in its way. I could maybe get hold of three hundred."

"Seven hundred," said Jimmy quickly.

"Make it five, and a trip to Chattanooga. If you can be ready to leave right away."

"We got nuthin' to pack."

"Stay right here in the car. I'll be ready in fifteen minutes." Then he added, "Part of the bargain is that the Sheriff does not know that you're gone."

125

"—Me tell the Law? No way. The less the Law," his voice made the word upper case, "knows what ahm' doin' . . . we wouldn' a' gotten eev–ac–you–ated if we hadn' gone in for welfare."

It would be at least a three hour trip each way. Craig put three empty five gallon cans in the back of the car. He'd fill them at the first station to hedge his luck. Then he headed into the house, hiding his jubilance, to tell Lex the news.

"I'll get some things on and go with you," she said as he reached in the top drawer of his dresser to get out a small pistol. "There might be trouble."

"No way," he told her fiercely. "I'll drop you at the foot of Jeff and Terry's drive. You can walk up. Oh, I forgot to tell you. They've got evacuees too. Two Mexican babies whose parent were killed . . . ."

"Babies! Craig! Why didn't you tell me?"

He grinned down at her, companionably. "We're about to get rid of the worst trouble I can imagine. One that would have destroyed what we are trying to build, in the long run. I would have had to get rid of them somehow, but outside of accidents in the woods I hadn't figured how. It was . . . ."

Lex's voice was angry. "We didn't have to get rid of them. Being up here with us and our ethics would have changed them. People can change, you know. And they'd have been a help, once they got strong. We will need strong, young bodies. Accidents in the woods!"

Craig shut his mouth, but her voice continued. "I just don't understand you any more," she said. "Babies . . . and they just slipped your mind! And you don't see the potential in people just because they're dirty and disreputable at the moment . . . ."

It was almost night before he was back from Chattanooga. Alone. He drove up the mountain to his son's house, readying himself to face whatever problems were up there.

He knocked lightly and opened the door.

Lex was holding an infant on her lap. A tiny boy was sturdily trying to climb a chair, Julie and Shamus daring him on. The room was scattered with baby things. Terry was fixing dinner.

"Oh, Craig," Lex looked up at him, her face a study in warm happiness, "the babies are so soft and cuddly, even though they're so <u>thin</u>."

"I think the boy is about eighteen months," Terry chimed in, "and the baby can't be more than two months. She's a girl. I don't dare name them in case some relatives who know their right names come to claim them. Their parents were working in a field near the plant and were killed."

He moved some toys from the nearest chair and sat down. All the way to Chattanooga and back he had worried at what he would find. His relief was a tangible thing.

He looked at his wife and daughter–in–law, still chattering, happy and busy. Babies have an attraction all their own, he told himself. If they didn't the race would have ended long ago.

But—this was no world in which to bring up babies. It was going to be hard enough for the adults to survive.

Then he asked himself, —or is it? If . . . if we're to have any future at all . . .?

But—Mexican? A different race? Different genetics? As if that mattered. It's the human race that is at hazard right now. There's an atavism about racism, he thought, about anything different. You think it's gone until it comes into your family, then it wells up from the depths, and you have to take a good new look and remember the likenesses and forget the differences. if there really are any.

He looked at Lex, the baby in her lap, its rosebud mouth slightly open; the long black eyelashes tight against its tan cheeks. He wanted to stroke the soft skin, but that might wake it. Instead, he walked over and kissed the top of Lex's head.

"We call them Uno and Dos, until we find out their names," Terry was saying happily. "Dos is the girl. That's about the extent of my Spanish." She laughed. "Uno calls me `Mamma.' I gather it's the same word in Mexican."

Craig walked over and fixed himself a drink, then settled comfortably in the chair he'd cleared. He pulled out a cigar and lit it.

He could relax now. For the moment at least.

The dogs began barking furiously. They listened as a motor sounded coming up the drive.

Craig jumped to his feet, took down a shotgun where it lay on a tall shelf out of the children's way. Then went out on the deck.

Carefully, Lex put the baby on the couch, saw to it that the older children were ready to catch Uno if he fell, then lifted down a .22 from the same shelf and went to stand behind her husband. Terry produced a pistol, and joined them.

"It's a motorcycle," Craig said as they listened. "You two stay out of the way until we see what's up this time."

The night was dark with clouds. The first small gusts of wind were making themselves felt.

Craig held the gun behind him where it wouldn't be seen. Terry positioned herself behind a drape at one window, Lex at the other. Jeff was probably coming quietly up from the barn, and would go in the back door, unseen.

They waited. Finally the cycle rounded the curve and neared the house.

There were two riders, both in helmets and gloves. The driver put the cycle on park, then reached back to help the smaller figure of a girl off.

She was obviously very pregnant, and as she pulled off her helmet, her dark skin—a deep, soft brown—was beneath a cropped head of tight black curls. Her face was gaunt, and she staggered a bit as she got her feet onto the ground.

Lex put her gun back on the shelf and ran out towards the girl, but Craig held her back.

The man, shucking his helmet and gloves, was even darker-skinned. About thirty, Craig guessed. He was powerfully built, a little over six feet. When he smiled, tentatively, it was a wary smile.

The woman started to step forward, but she staggered again, and Lex pushed past her husband's restraining hand to go to her, taking her arm.

"I'm looking for work," the man said. His voice was deep but cautious. "I can put a hand to most anything, from chopping wood to carpentry to mechanics. We may be radioactive," he added. "We were about fifty miles away from our home near Oconee when it blew, but we didn't go back. We've always lived away from people. I don't think we've been exposed to anything."

The wind gusted again, harder this time. In the distance lightning sheeted, and they could hear the rumble of thunder.

Craig put his shotgun down behind the door, then picked it up again and put it on the high shelf. Jeff appeared at the back of the room, and Craig flashed him an `okay signal, as he went out to the couple in the drive. These, he thought, are our kind of people.

"You'd better come on in," he told them. "You look beat."

"They may be covered with fallout," Lex said. "We mustn't expose the babies. We'll take them to our place."

"You've got nothing against blacks?" The man's voice was less cautious, his manner gentle. "Down the road they don't cotton to our color. If you care about color, we'll be on our way."

Lex smiled, and Craig realized that she liked this couple as much as he did.

"I've never noticed any real differences," she said, "but the people around here aren't used to your kind. There are very few in the area. We do admire people with a variety of abilities." Then she added, "Your wife shouldn't be riding a motorcycle so near term."

The lightning was getting closer, the wind gusting harder.

"My name is Amos. Amos Thompson. And my wife is Harriet." His smile brightened his whole face, which was smooth and almost round.

Lex offered her hand to each in turn, and Craig followed suit.

If we have evacuees in residence, Craig thought, nobody can push any more on us. Even if they find out the others are gone.

"This is my son's house," he said. "They have four babies in residence, and my wife is right. We shouldn't take you inside until the fallout's gone. We'll go up to our place."

"Harriet will ride with us." Lex turned to the girl. "You really shouldn't be riding a cycle now. Amos can bring it along behind."

"I wouldn't have let her ride, except that was the only way we could get away. The baby's due in two months." Amos' voice held a deep relief.

"I shouldn't get fallout in your car," Harriet said weakly. "It may have blown off?"

"It probably has. Don't worry about it."

The cabin was a mess. Lex cleared the bathrobes off a chair and seated Harriet in it firmly. Then she began to clear up dirty dishes.

"Let me do that, ma'am." Harriet was at her shoulder.

"My name is Lex. Alexandra Gallagher."

"Okay, Mrs. Gallagher." Harriet reached to take the dishes.

"Make it Lex, and now you sit down. We don't want you having that baby here and now? After you're rested . . . ."

Craig opened the stove to start a fire, but Amos moved in front of him. "I'm pretty good at tending stove," he said.

Outside the storm broke, lashing the cabin with rain, shaking it with wind, howling through the trees.

Amos was skillfully wadding paper and bark to give the fire a start. He looked up. "We've been having tornadoes in the Piedmont," he said cheerfully. "That wind sounds just as loud, but it's not twisting."

"The mountains break up tornadoes," Craig told him, pleased and beginning to feel relaxed. "But I think these winds are just as strong, only not focused to a point."

"You can take showers as soon as I can get these bathrobes and sheets washed and bring them back," Lex was telling Harriet as she wadded up the sheets from the beds. "It's an instant propane hot water system, so you don't have to wait for a tank to heat. It will take me about an hour. Then we can wash out your clothes. There's no washing machine down here, but we have one up at the house we can all use."

"I can wash them by hand."

"Why, when we've a washing machine?"

"But the . . . ." Abruptly the tears began flowing down Harriet's cheeks.

Lex went to the woman—scarcely more than a girl. "Oh, my dear," she said.

"You don't know." Harriet wiped the tears with her fingers. "You . . . you're making us welcome. And . . . this place is so lovely. It has all the old things . . . it's . . . ."

130

Craig slipped out of the room with a deep satisfaction. This was going to work.

Carolyn Armentrout arrived several days later.

It was a dark day. The wind was light, the mountains gray with haze. There had been an earthquake in Tennessee. They were getting closer.

Craig watched from the deck as the beat-up MG-B climbed the mountain, scraping its bottom on the ruts occasionally; scratching to climb the steep entrance.

The driver got out and came toward the house. To his astonishment, it was a girl—thin—slender, he corrected himself. She had a long stride that swung her hips nicely. Light brown hair to her shoulders, hanging loose around her face which was plain but pert. She stopped and looked around the mountains, and a smile broke out that made her almost beautiful, it was so spontaneous and delighted.

Craig went out to meet her.

"I think my uncle has a cabin up here," she told him. "I'm Carol Armentrout. You must be Mr. Gallagher. I read your wife's book. It's terrific."

Craig held out his hand, and the rapport was immediate. He was fond of the Armentrouts, had admired the way they had restored the old cabin. The niece, he decided, was like them.

Lex came out and he introduced them, while he considered the problem.

The cabin belonged to the Armentrouts. But what were the privileges of ownership now, with the civilization falling apart?

He shook himself. The old order changeth, he told himself; but all our obligations are not lifted. At least, not yet. So quickly is our mountain filling with refugees! Yet, so quickly is our world disintegrating.

"We'll bring Harriet and Amos up here," he told Lex quietly.

She turned to the newcomer. "We're glad to see you," she said. "Were you near the Oconee disaster?"

She laughed. "No," she answered. "I was living in Philadelphia. I've known for months that I should get out of the city— come up here— but I didn't really believe myself. Told myself I didn't believe in hunches; that I certainly didn't act on them.

131

"Then everybody and his brother began getting the flu or being robbed or mugged. A couple of my friends were killed. It was getting rough, but me, I figured I was rugged. Then a girl down the way got broken and entered while she was out, and her apartment trashed. The scene was getting too rancid, even for me. So I got on my hunch and came."

Lex nodded. Then: "We've taken advantage of your uncle," she said. "We put a couple of evacuees in the old log cabin. But we'll move them up to this house right away, and I can have the place ready for you in a few hours."

Carol looked at Lex strangely. "Evacuees? I'd heard that evacuees were being placed around the country . . . ."

Lex nodded. "These two are sort of unofficial. The first ones we got here were quite official, delivered by the National Guard. Drug addicts," she added. "When they couldn't supply themselves with drugs here, they got Craig to take them to Chattanooga.

"So when this couple arrived on their own motorcycle and without being brought by," she chuckled, "by the Law . . . why we took them in right now. They're clean and quite able people, besides being warm and good. I'll take you down now and introduce you, give them the news. That's your uncle's cabin down there."

Carol looked down the mountain at the cabin, smoke coming from its chimney, Amos outside chain-sawing wood for the winter. It looked peaceful. Her face fell. "I'd hate to dispossess . . . I could find somewhere else. Even if my hunch did say here . . . .?"

"It's your cabin," Craig said firmly. We'll bring them up here. They can have our guest room."

He heard his voice, assured. Inside he was distressed. Harriet and Amos fitted so well, and with the baby coming they needed their own space. Never mind, he told himself, it's a minor problem compared to . . . . He didn't finish the thought.

"Maybe I could just move in with them?" Carol looked around at the huge great room they were in; at the meadow beneath the window; at the long vista down the cove.

"This is lovely," she said. "Who owns the meadow? Maybe I could put a tent down there? I could get a big one. It might be an eyesore . . . ."

Craig felt his worries subsiding. She was no clinging vine.

So many things were changing, as though by themselves. This change might be for the better, granted the circumstances.

"Wouldn't you rather stay with us?" Lex would solve the problem, Craig decided. He'd rather that they could be alone, but that was obviously going to be impossible. "You could be our evacuee," Lex was prattling on. "Then nobody could put any more people up here. Besides, I'm a good cook. But then, so is Harriet."

Carol smiled at her. "Let me talk to them first," she said.

They walked down, Carol with her long, springy stride as though she were used to the mountains. At first she held back, staying beside them, then abruptly ran down the hill.

Amos looked up as the newcomer approached, and Carol held out her hand. "I'm Carol Armentrout," she said.

"Hello. I saw you drive up to the Gallagher's. I was surprised your tiny MG could make it. I'm Amos Thompson." Then, as Harriet came to the door, drying her hands on a dishtowel, "This is my wife, Harriet."

Carol shook her hand, then asked, "When is it due?"

She smiled shyly. "Almost two months yet. It's our first. Won't you come in?"

By then the Gallaghers had reached the cabin, and the four went in. "I'll be along in a minute," Amos told them.

The cabin was warm and cozy and clean. Carol looked around admiringly. Harriet left to get coffee. "I always have it on the stove," she said. "I'm getting real good at a wood stove."

Carol turned to Lex. "May I be your evacuee?" she asked softly. "They need the space with the baby coming. But maybe you need the space too?"

"Please," she was answered. "We'd be so delighted. You've no idea. You don't mind them having your cabin?"

"Don't tell them it's mine . . . or rather, my uncle's. It might embarrass them. They seem swell." Then she added, "I don't have much money to pay room and board. I was expecting to live in Uncle's cabin on nothing but what I could scrounge for myself."

Craig interrupted. "None of us has much money," he said. "Lex and I have spent almost all of ours making this place . . . ." he gestured around at the mountains . . . "safe. We'll all scrounge. Anyhow, we're expected to support our evacuees."

133

It was true, he thought. Their money was nearly gone. But there was food in the larder—possibly enough for a running start with so big a family—and propane. It was time to start filling the gasoline barrels they had buried . . . .

Lex was smiling contentedly. "We're a real family now," she said. "There are my son and daughter-in-law, with two children of their own and two honest-to-God Mexican baby evacuees, brought by the Armed Services. They've turned out to be wonderful.

"Then there are these two and their coming baby. And you. Of course Craig and myself. Oh, and Yuri, up a ways, our resident electronic genius. How many is that?"

"Thirteen," Craig said. "The Witching number." He put his arm around his wife's slender waist and squeezed gently.

"And you," he continued, smiling down at her fondly, "You are the Good Witch, brewing cauldrons of love and warmth and ethics. And I shall guard your cauldrons from those who have become degraded, though you learn to hate me for it."

INTERLUDE

The entire body of the Earth was quivering now, almost without let–up.

Her skin was tight, leprous. Her coatings of trees and grasses had been pulled off in great swatches. Nearly constant fires burned on her surface.

Inside was agony. Her nervous system was becoming disfunctional under the constant, increasing electronic arrows shooting pains through her body and around her.

The normal magnetic flux in the areas where the sun's newly vicious magnetic fields touched and crossed her own, were enlarging, creating new melt to spout to and through her surface. Her substructure of melt was writhing, seemed to distend, to contract, to shift, to change.

Her innermost self was contracting. Deep quakes beneath her oceans sent her waters breaking over the land. She could feel convulsions above and below he surface.

She was spouting gases and golden melt almost constantly. Her waters were obscene with refuse; the atmosphere around her was changed to unseemly fog. Monster hurricanes formed and swept her surface.

She was shuddering constantly now—gigantic shudders that moved even the granite plates that shelled her surface.

She was reaching a crisis that bid fair to tear her asunder.

12

The sun was barely up next morning, when Craig reached the living room. It was chilly. Soon they'd have to start the stove. For now, he turned on the electric strip–heaters in the great room, and put water on for coffee.

Lex appeared as the coffee water reached a boil, and almost at the same moment Carol erupted from the guest room. It wasn't an intentional eruption, Craig decided as the girl flung herself at the two of them, giving each a hug. It was just what was probably the energy and delight with which she normally greeted a day.

"Coffee?"

"Breakfast shortly," Lex told her, her smile nearly as broad as the girl's.

It was a gay meal. Craig had nearly forgotten the spontaneity with which his own teenagers had once filled their home.

"What's on the agenda for today?" Carol asked as she cleared the table and began washing dishes. "If it's nothing you need me for, I think I'll go up and meet our resident infidel."

An hour later Carol and Yuri appeared together. Yuri wasted no time in greetings.

"Carol tells me you've had some unpleasant invaders," he said. " I don't mean the guys bringing evacuees, but raiders."

Craig was fascinated by the young man's face. It seemed different. Why, the "grim" was gone, he realized. His whole face was interested and alight.

"Yeah," he said laconically. "Once or twice. We've had a light beam signal put across the neck of the cove road. At least it gives us warning."

Yuri grinned. Carol was smothering a laugh in the background.

"You _are_ prehistoric electronically," he said. I'll put a fear signal down there that no one will come through."

"A fear signal?"

"An ultra low frequency signal in the fear cycle. It'll scare the bejesus out of anyone. They'll turn and run."

"What," asked Craig, "is a fear cycle?"

136

"Oh, that's DEM electronics. You've been subject to it in a sort of dispersed manner, sporadically, for a long time. Both the big governments, and probably a batch of the smaller ones have been dosing us with it to soften everybody up for several years now. You remember when the American Embassy in Russia was being attacked by electronic sabotage? That was near the beginning. It's gotten more effective over the years. California was one of the test cases for a while.

"This whole planet—the universe, in fact—is a huge EM/DEM system."

At Craig's questioning look, he explained: "EM—electromagnetic. DEM—dielectric/diamagnetic. The opposed system. Now that we've got the DEM half, it's a whole new world. Those that are psionically sophisticated can handle it, even though they don't know what they're handling. Those that aren't, can't."

"Psionically?"

"You know. The field. The spirit. The soul. We've been calling it all sorts of names because we knew we had it but we didn't know what it was or how to use it. It's the other half of you. The dielectric/diamagnetic half. Easy way to say it is DEM.

"You've noticed that people are sort of dividing up these days? The ones who can handle the DEM and the ones who can't? And never the twain shall meet. You watch. You'll see."

He turned away. Then turned back. "I'll get that fear cycle going at the neck of the cove. Then we won't be bothered. And by the way, Carol is moving up with me."

Carol giggled and turned to Lex, who had sat listening.

"You don't mind? I'll get my stuff."

Craig watched vaguely as the girl headed into the guest room. The soul. The spirit, Dielectrics. Diamagnetics. What in hell did that have anything to do with the nuts and bolts of the world? Religion? It didn't sound like it. Nuts, he thought, and then chuckled to himself. And bolts. He'd settle for that.

As soon as the kids were gone, he'd head into town. It was time to fill the gasoline barrels. They had held off as long as possible, since gasoline only had an eighteen month shelf life; but the time had gone. Actually, he'd only have to go as far as the truck stop off the thruway, he realized.

"I'll go with you," Lex said when she realized what he was doing.

"No," he answered. "It's rough out there these days, and a female of the species is at more hazard than the male. I'll drop you at Jeff's."

"I don't like being left out of the adventures." Lex was really put out.

He smiled at her fondly. "I'm being a chauvinistic pig," he told her, "but I need to be free to . . . take care of any emergencies."

"I'll stay here and work on the book," she said finally. "With Harriet and Amos down the hill, and Yuri and Carol up, I should be safe from the . . . baarrs."

Craig loaded up the three jerry cans he had, then headed for Jeff's where he traded for the pickup and added three more jerry cans. It would take four trips to the truck stop to fill the barrels. Not as much gasoline as he'd like to store, but . . . well, enough for a running start no matter what happened. It would keep the chain saws supplied at least, and maybe some for vehicles. They'd use one barrel at a time, and replace with fresh as long as possible.

He headed down the cove, around the first hair–pin curve, and found terror clutching at his entrails. Panic. Just around the corner there would be . . . he had to get back . . . had to get home . . . .

He was sweating, his hands on the steering wheel slippery. There was no place to turn around. They'd get him. His legs began shaking, and he could hardly hold his foot on the accelerator. He was going too fast, but he couldn't stop. Run . . . he had to run. Get out of the truck and . . . .

Abruptly the terror was gone. He had reached the paved road at the foot of the cove. He pulled to the side of the road and sat there shaking.

What in hell . . . he'd never been so scared. It was stupid. Unreasonable.

Slowly the shaking subsided, and his intelligence returned.

He slid down in the seat and let himself relax. Fear, out of nowhere. Fear that had overcome his innate sanity and gripped him by the throat until he could no longer think.

Fear. The fear cycle. That had to be it. Yuri had said . . . . But what a revelation!

The truck stop was a few miles down the way, and he set the pickup in motion, furious now.

Orson Welles and his invasion from Mars. He'd heard that Welles had had a fear cycle underneath. People had panicked at a dull radio show . . . run into the streets, trying to get away. All over New Jersey. Maybe the signal didn't reach much further? Afterwards, when they'd played it again, it was just dull. The fear cycle was not there. Nobody panicked, and nobody was able to understand.

Had it been the crucial factor when the Israelis took the impregnable Golan Heights during their five day war? Their soldiers had stormed the Heights twice, been thrown back by withering fire. The third time they stormed they'd been accompanied by fanfares of ramshorns—and the defenders had fled even before they reached the strongholds.

Both had been years ago. He'd noted the facts at the time but tossed them aside as simply unusual factors.

He filled the jerry cans at the truck stop, then headed for their pay phone, dialing Yuri's place.

It was Carol who answered, and she was giggling. He swallowed his fury.

"Yuri says he'll turn it off for you to get back," she told him. "It worked?"

"Just tell him I'll smash his head in . . . No, I won't. He's right. We won't be invaded. I guess . . . well, I guess you can tell him thanks.

"But you two get on down to my house. I'm coming right back and I want to talk to him."

Carol was looking smug when Craig walked in; Yuri was drinking coffee with Lex at the table.

"Think you're safe now?" Yuri asked.

"Old Merlin here has the neatest magic," Carol interposed before Craig could reply. "He's going to teach me."

"That one was real concentrated," Yuri said. "The ones the governments use are broader, more diluted. You don't notice them as much."

Craig went to the cupboard and got out a bottle. He still wasn't quite over the shakes. He poured himself a drink, but didn't offer any to the others. Glass in hand, he walked over to the table and sat down.

"It was quite an experience," he admitted. "Quite. Now I need to know what else you can do with that magic of yours besides scaring the pants off people."

"Oh, it's very practical stuff." Yuri's face and voice were serious. "Everything has two halves, equals but opposed. The DEM cycle—the time cycle—is the patterning part. It is a field, around and through the physical. EM is the physical part. It follows the pattern. It's the demonstration of the pattern. You change the DEM pattern, the EM changes to suit.

"There are farmers using it—not many but enough to prove the point. They use it to clean up the soil, grow healthy plants, and the bottom line bears them out."

Craig was startled. "Hadn't heard of it," he said.

"Not many have. It takes intelligence and training. And the equipment if fairly costly. I can also," Yuri continued, "set fire to a barn in Istanbul, or explode a plane over the Atlantic. Or make people nervous in California. The governments—mostly—are playing with that part, but their generals don't believe 'em and stick to conventionals." He was winding down.

Craig leaned back in his chair. He needed that drink, he decided, as much to confront this . . . magician . . . as to counter the effects of the panic he'd had. If I hadn't felt the results of some of this work, I wouldn't believe a word of this, he realized. But that panic was real.

"Okay," he said. "Now. Just what is this DEM? Remember I'm an amateur. If I hadn't just been through your "gate"—Have you put it back?"

"Not yet, but I will."

"Jesus. Wait till a stranger tries to come in! Now, what is it?"

"You're so used to dealing with the world of the five senses. Why you can't even detect radar with those five senses! I'll try.

"Take alternating current electricity. The electricity flows until it builds up a wall of magnetic flux; at right angles to itself, at which point it collapses. As it collapses, it creates a dielectric current at right angles both to itself and to the magnetic field.

"Now the magnetic field in its turn expands, creating an electric current at right angles to itself, then collapses. As it collapses, it creates a diamagnetic field at right angles both to itself and to the electric field.

"The solid EM half of you—what you consider real you recognize with its five senses.

"The other half of you—invisible to those five senses—is a field circulating in and through the solid half, with its own brain and its own senses; and its own holographic memory and information storage.

"We've been calling the DEM half the spirit, the soul, psionics, what you will, because we didn't know what it was. Sure you want me to tell you all this?"

"You see?" Carol giggled. "It's pure magic. And he's Merlin."

Craig stood up and began to pace the floor. Lex refilled the coffee cups.

"I'm going to have to take it on faith," he said finally. "Maybe we'd better let it go at that for now. Later, maybe you could take me on as a kindergartner? Teach me some of what it is you're talking about?"

"Oh, you could learn to use it. It's the basic principles that are tough. To understand, this is."

"Are many people using this stuff?"

"Besides some farmers and some governments? I've got friends all over the planet. Have to wait till the winds stop and I can put up my ham tower to get back in touch with them. It takes intelligence to run the equipment, so they're not just run–of–the–mill types. But there are quite a number of them. Language is a problem, but not much. Most of them know English, and I was born in Czechoslovakia and lived in China for years. My father was a missionary. So I get along with most of them." He stood up and turned to the door, followed by Carol. At the door he turned.

"DEM. You don't have to understand it. Just relax with it." Then he added, "Carol's moved in with me. You don't have to understand that either." He grinned. Carol giggled.

As the door closed, Craig turned to Lex. "You should have felt it! It was unbelievable! `You call it the soul . . . .' Yuri said. Nuts. It was the realest fear possible."

He turned to the phone. "We'd better warn any friend who might be coming up to let us know so we can get Yuri to turn the damned thing off. I'll phone Jim Lord, Jeff's friend, the one who warned us about the gangs."

The voice that answered was gruff, that of a stranger.

"May I speak to Jim Lord? Craig asked.

There was a bellow of laughter, then: "He's gone. We live here now."

"Where can I find him? Who are you?"

The man was still chortling. "I don' know and I don' care where he got to. This's our place now. And you wouldn' know me. Me and a bunch cut out of Atlanta when things got rough. Decided this was the place for us. Nice, comfortable, food in the fridge. You gotta nice place too? I got friends . . . ."

* * *

October opened brilliant and hot, as hot as a normal August, even in the mountains.

Then came the late hurricanes. The biggest swept out of the South Atlantic and hit around Chesapeake Bay, crashing its way up the coast instead of going inland to dissipate itself over land. A second followed it, heading into the Yucatan Peninsula and into Mexico, where giant mudslides made anything hitherto seem like children's mudpies. Huge typhoons wrecked the Philippines and Japan.

Quakes of seven, eight and nine Richter were no longer uncommon. California had been hit again and again, but San Francisco was spared anything really devastating . . . but it was coming . . . it was coming. Alaska had been severely shaken, and Anchorage and the peninsula were disaster areas.

Japan suffered again, but withstood the quakes with relatively minor damage and death. China and Asia as a whole underwent massive destruction.

And always the winds . . . .

It was the earthquake that finally hit the central Carolinas that did the damage in their cove. They were far from the epicenter, but the houses shook, the trees swayed, dishes crashed from the shelves.

Craig, Jeff and Terry were in the downahill house when it hit, were knocked to the floor, dishes and pans cascading around

142

them. As soon as they could stand they all headed to the door, to meet Shamus and Julie running in.

The two children were shaking, and Terry took them in her arms. Shamus lifted a brave face to her, a cut on his face streaming blood.

"I knew it was coming," he said, "and I made Julie lie down in the grass. But I knew that Maggie would fall down and get hurt, so I tried to get to her."

His voice held a sob. "I couldn't get to her in time, and she fell down," he said. "I think she's hurt. The other horses," he said, "are all right. It was just Maggie that was going to fall down."

"I did what Shamus said," Julie put in tearfully. "You'd told us to. I lay down. I didn't get hurt. Much," she added.

Jeff was kneeling beside Terry and the children. Craig went to the telephone. It still worked, to his surprise. He dialed Lex, to find her shaken but undaunted. "My computer danced," she said, "but I grabbed it and it didn't fall. I guess it held me from falling."

"Go see about Maggie," Shamus insisted. "She's hurt."

"Okay," said Jeff. "But you kids stay here. There may be aftershocks."

As they got near the barn they could see three of the horses standing, but one was down, struggling. Jeff broke into a run.

When Craig reached his son, he was kneeling beside the mare, his face averted. "Leg's broken," he said, his voice harsh. "We'll have to shoot her."

He shook his head, swallowing. "Thank God it wasn't one of the children." His voice was shaking. "Will you get my forty–five. And tell Terry. She'll be heartbroken, but don't let her come out."

"I'll call Yuri to give us a hand." Craig kept his voice even. "Time he got into the family."

Terry broke into sobs, holding the children close. She looked up at her father-in-law. "I have to do it myself," she said. "You have to shoot your own dog."

"No," said Craig firmly. "You have to take care of your own children. That's your first job. The rest—we'll handle."

Jeff had his emotions under control by the time Craig got back. Yuri was driving up in his pickup as the shot was fired, the beautiful animal relaxing in death. His face was grim, but not the same grim, Craig decided. He had the look of being determinedly practical . . . and that's a necessary ingredient, Craig thought.

Yuri stood looking at the scene without a word, then went to the back of his pickup and pulled out a tow belt. He patted Jeff's shoulder as he passed. "Damned world," he said shortly, then looked over the problem.

"We'll have to tow from the rear," he said firmly. "The head would be too wobbly."

It took them an hour to get the tow belt under the animal, to fasten heavy ropes to increase its length, to attach it to the pickup. The ground shuddered a few times while they worked, but it was only shudders.

The three were almost silent, working together. Yuri's strength is phenomenal, Craig thought. As they finally tightened the hitch, Yuri climbed into the driver's seat.

"Where?" he asked.

Jeff answered. "There's an old lumber trail leads over the ridge. That would take it out of sight. For the kids," he added.

Craig turned to the old trail ahead of them, his long strides eating the distance. He hadn't explored here yet, but the trail was fairly clear.

By the time the truck with its unwieldy burden came over the ridge he had found what he was looking for—a hollow big enough.

They maneuvered the big body in, took turns shoveling dirt and rocks over it, hiding it as best they could.

"That will have to do," said Craig finally. "Our first complete casualty. We can't afford to mourn, or let the gals mourn," he told the other two. "There'll be too much to mourn over in the future.

"We can't let ourselves, or them—or the children—spend too much emotion on this, We have to be adamant."

INTERLUDE

The Earth felt gravid.

Her plates, beneath her outer crust, were fluttering, trying to stretch against the roilings of her center.

Her crust was rupturing from the magnetic flux points that came and went and changed.

Her rotation was slowing in consistent microseconds, magnetic brakes pitted against the inertial force of her volume.

Her atmosphere brawled with a turbulence that uprooted the furs of her surface.

Her waters were smashing against her coastlines, trying to break free . . . .

13

Mid October. The mountains became a blaze of glory. First the yellows of the poplars, brown of the sycamores, maroons of the berry bushes and sumac, as the woods dressed themselves as for a farewell party to a most unusual summer.

Then came the reds of the maples, brilliant against the green of fir and pine; and the deep brown–reds of the oak.

The violence of the weather abated as though in respect for the festival. Earthquakes elsewhere were an almost daily news item, but so far no more in the east.

Kathy and Brian were coming. Only for two days, but "Maybe they'll decide to stay," Lex said hopefully. "They're driving. They'll be safe enough . . . ."

"Probably," Craig agreed. "About their staying. I hope they will. But—remember everybody, even our own children, have to make up their own minds. Have to look at the evidence, make their own decisions."

They would make it a party—a celebration. With decorations, the children decided.

Shamus and Julie, in charge of those decorations, decided to make paper chains. They had no kraft paper, so they got out old Penney's and Sears catalogs, cutting the colorful paper into strips, making flour and water paste, creating both chains and a great mess.

It was a glorious two days. Kathy's laughter filled the house; Brian was a big bear, exploring and admiring all the things they had done, the preparations they had made.

On the last day everybody crowded into the Uppahill house for a feast. Lex had gotten a turkey from the freezer, and the fixin's of potatoes and carrots and onions from the root cellar. She got cranberry sauce from their store of canned goods; and mixed up extra dried milk for gravy and a cake.

While Lex, Terry and Carol cooked up a storm, Harriet took over the care of the smallfry, Julie hung the pasty–chains, and Kathy sat on the dining table with a guitar, her feet on a chair, playing and singing ribald songs in which the others joined.

Brian, holding Shamus by the hand, led the men to the wood–pile to "show off my skill with an axe." He clowned awkwardness

146

for minutes until he had Craig, Jeff, Amos and Yuri in stitches, then began splitting the logs as though he had been born to it.

Dinner was a magnificent affair; and afterwards Craig got out a bottle of brandy, solemnly pouring the drinks, including bits for the children.

"What are we drinking to?" Brian asked, raising his glass.

"To being alive and able to celebrate," Craig said solemnly. "To being on our mountain, at least a bit removed from the chaos."

Shortly Amos and Harriet offered to bed the children in their cabin so their elders could have a last evening together.

Craig refilled the glasses, lit a cigar and leaned back in his chair.

He turned to his son–in–law. "We're hoping you'll join us up here," he said. "It's pretty grim out."

Brian laughed. "I can't imagine Kathy in this setting," he answered. "Anyhow, it will blow over. The Para will work itself out. In New York and Tampa, people are making do until the crisis is past. Life goes on, and people find a way. They always have."

"You're making yourselves part of the other half," Yuri said.

"Other half?" Brian's question was light.

"The other half. Too civilized to see what's happening and adapt. The after–birth," Yuri muttered. Abruptly, "You don't need a ghoul at the feast," he said. "We'd better get back to the house. C'mon Carol. It was good meeting you," the two chorused as they left.

The women began to clear the table, started the dish washing. By hand. Dishwashers were extraneous, they had long since decided.

Craig took a sip of his brandy. "I'd like, at least, to show you how to get here safely, if you change your minds?"

Brian shook his head. "Your young misanthropist may be right, that Kathy and I are too civilized. But things can't get much worse. We've hit bottom and it will start to turn around now."

"But just in case?"

Brian began to pay attention at last. "If it were anybody but you, I'd say you were nuts." He shrugged. "You're looking at a worst case scenario. Kathy and I are trying to get people to change their environmental ways before it's too late."

"Assume that we're past the point of no return?"

Brian laughed. "People will find a way to cope. They always have. However, you're obviously sincere. Will you . . . show me the way to go home?"

At least he's going to listen, Craig thought, leaning forward, centering Brian's attention with his gaze. If things get to the worst, maybe he'll bring our Busy Bee and get to us.

"The first thing," he said, "is to get away from the megapolis as fast as possible. That's where the greatest dangers are. From Tampa . . . ."

Brian smiled. He's placating me, Craig thought. He's looking at the problems as though somebody could wave a wand and they'd go away. I hope he's right; but I hope he remembers what I'm saying . . . in case.

He could see his baby, his Busy Bee as a child, her blond hair tossing, her laughing face turned up to him, her hand trustingly in his. He wanted to hold her in his arms again, protect her.

Safe in Daddy's arms? he scolded himself. How idiotic can I get. She's grown . . . and gone to her own world and its decisions.

* * *

In the kitchen area Lex, Terry and Kathy listened quietly while they worked until the conversation got to road directions, in lower tones.

Kathy looked at Lex, a long look. "We're betting on the other side, Mom," she said softly. "It's a gamble, you know. I couldn't bet against Brian even if I wanted to, which I don't. I like what you're doing here. Especially the Sunday planning and standards conferences Terry was telling me about . . . ."

"They get quite controversial," Lex said.

"Should be. You don't set standards and plans without looking at all perspectives." She hugged Lex quickly, one–armed. "But Mom, I like the bet Brian and I are making. I'd rather bet for the human race than against it."

Lex looked her daughter in the eye. "We're betting <u>for</u> the human race in our own way," she said fiercely. "It's a life or death gamble the human race is facing.

"You're betting you can change the nature of the whole race—men, women and children—in every nation of the world—without too many starving or being killed—and can change them in time so they rebuild their planet into a greenhouse.

"It's our bet that if we—and some others like us, hopefully a lot of others and spotted all over the planet—some of all races, creeds and colors—if we survive in spite of everything that is already happening—then the race will continue. If not, we don't think it will.

"And—if you should succeed and change the attitudes of the world today—not even tomorrow, but today—I think you're already too late."

* * *

The house was quiet except for lightning and thunder outside. The storms were back and constant, as though sensing that the holiday was over. Back with a violence that was almost a new characteristic.

Craig was at his side of the big desk when Lex headed for her word processor.

"It's time," she told him brightly, "that I got started on my next book—though I'm not sure who or what I'm writing it for."

"Perhaps our children's children?"

"Perhaps. It will be called `Humanity in Chaos.' I've got to understand the `civilized' attitude. Brian and Kathy. Trying to prop up the old structure that is falling down on top of them, rather than getting out of the way of the avalanche that is roaring down to demolish it completely . . . and then rebuilding. That's the question. Rebuilding. Can we?"

She switched on her computer, then turned to him again. "I'm not sure they really want to escape," she said. "A sort of go–down–with–the–ship thing. Until the last minute, of course."

She turned to the keys. Almost immediately words began to appear on the screen.

Instant writer, he thought. Her mind works on what she wants to say constantly—sometimes underneath, sometimes on top, and she make notes on paper.

When she sits down to the keyboard, it begins to flood out. First draft. Then second—over and over, until she gets what she wants. Always through to the end, on each draft.

He shook his head. Not the violence outside nor any comings and goings bothered her. Writing, she was in a world to herself.

He pulled the desk calendar to him, recorded the weather for the day in the upper left hand corner of the page. Temperature, sixty degrees. Lightning and thunder, lashing rain. Two inches in the last twenty-four hours. Earthquakes on the east coast, 3.6 and 4.5 Richter. In Alabama and California, 5.3 and 6.7 Richter.

He looked at it thoughtfully. If I can continue to keep this daily record through thick and thin, then we'll eventually have comparative figures for the years.

But those figures don't show the fear when the winds howl almost up to three figures. They don't underline the inadequacy you feel as you watch TV, as you look at what is happening. They don't show the need to put screens around your family, to hold close to everything that has been dear, to protect and plan to protect those you love.

I'll need a running commentary too, he determined. A diary? Sort of. Plans and thoughts and comments. A form of letter to the grandchildren when they grow up.

He pulled his keyboard into position, then sat looking down the long valley towards the distant mountain range.

"There was a science fiction story I read once," he wrote, "called The Year of the Jackpot.

"The hero kept track of all the crazy things happening on earth and made charts. He decided that they would all culminate that year, at one time. And sure enough they did—in the book. He ended with the sun going nova, which seemed to me a bit extreme.

"Yet I watch what I see happening and I cling—rather desperately, I'm afraid—to Lex's idea that this may be the birth of a new civilization; and the parts that are being destroyed are the afterbirth.

"That would be comforting. Something wonderful coming out of all this violence and chaos. That the violence is not essentially destruction, but the terrifying contractions, the labor pains, of a new civilization being born. A civilization conceived nearly six thousand years ago.

"I had never before thought of how the fetus must feel when labor begins; only of the mother.

"But the fetus—with little if any warning at all, finds itself being torn apart, as we are being torn apart. Separated from its support structure. Twisted and turned and squeezed to the ultimate before it is thrust violently into a new world.

"To it, the new world must seem horrendous—lights, brilliant lights pouring into eyes that had always been in blackness. Being bandied about and spanked, squalling its first breaths into its lungs; being measured and washed and dressed and then put all by itself into a place where there is no reassuring mother's heartbeat, none of the wonderful quiet and surrounding strengths in which it grew.

"Lex says that the only thing that is truly predictable is the approximate time for the termination of a pregnancy. She says that this, that seems to us like the end of the civilized world, has been predicted for thousands of years, which could be the extent of a planetary pregnancy, figured in planetary time.

"She says that the Mayans put the gestation period for a civilization at 5,920 years . . . from the Neolithic to birth; that the first clay writing tablets, found at Sumer, were made 5,000 years ago.

"That is the anthropologist speaking.

"I quite hope that she is right; that there is reason and a future to the dissolution around us. That it makes sense in the long run—the incredible number of wars and revolutions and riots and poisons. Would those poisons be—those buried wastes, the pollution—would they be, comparably, the pituitrin that floods the mother's system to bring on the birth cycle?

"I don't know. I can only hope that, in this case, the end justifies the means, whether intentionally or as a spontaneous and inevitable part of reproduction."

He paused, then went on with his writing. "We each live in a type of isolation, our lives encompassed by our own problems, our own space–limits. Our own privacy. Each within ourselves.

"This is a necessity. Were we to open our hearts and minds completely to the people and events—even those nearest us—that do not directly affect our lives, we should be overwhelmed.

"A little we can give, emotionally and of our time and our means. But only a little, compared to the vast swings of events and emotions and needs across the planet.

151

"It is nearly impossible to comprehend, much less to spend emotional strength, on all the enormous panorama of forces that are sweeping the world—the starving, the abused, the abased, the drugged, the victims of earthquake and flood, the victims of weather, the high, the low, the government, the governed, taxes, crime . . . .

"'Pick a Cause and March' has become the watchword. A cause—any one cause—on which to expend the strengths and passions that are demanded daily, hourly, on TV, on radio, from the pulpit, from the speaker's platform. One cause to satisfy the conscience.

"The forces are cumulative; the needs are cumulative; yet it is nearly impossible to add them, coldly and accurately, and to draw conclusions from the whole of mankind, now that mankind has become a whole, its nervous system, its communications, encompassing the globe.

"You look at the pattern that you see, as the accumulation of events grows; and then you look at what is happening around you, and it is the same old world, the same problems as yesterday; the same sun shining.

"Yet, I remember something that John MacDonald wrote: 'Somewhere there are intelligent and highly skilled design engineers working the bugs out of ever more deadly weapons—lasers to blind armies; multiple multiple warheads; flames that stick to flesh and can't be extinguished; heat beams to fry crews inside their tanks.

"'And they pack up the printouts and turn off the computers and have a knock with the guys on the way home to the kiddies. Somebody has to do it. Right?'

"Yet where you sit, nothing much is changed. The winds blow high, the earthquakes increase, the potential of bombs sits on your shoulders, here and there a nuclear plant melts down, trucks with acid spills—but you eat three meals a day and watch TV at night to see what's happening. So you shrug and decide maybe you're right, maybe you're wrong, but who cares?

"There's not enough caring left over after the day to day caring about eating and sleeping and debts and where–is–the–money–coming–from and whatever cause you've worked up a sweat over.

"Anyhow, what can you do? There's the job and the mortgage and the credit card to pay off.

"And you think of all the times a crazy sect has decided the world would end on a certain day, and you wonder what became of them after it didn't. But did it? Has our world already ended and we just haven't noticed?

"You watch the news, and listen to the derangement of the world . . . the nightly dish of catastrophe. Each event is too much; too big; and you look away.

"You also look away from the addition that spells destruction in our time. Immediate, in planetary terms. Within months. Or years.

"Or am I taking that half–step from reality that makes the world seem to bulge into strange shapes?

"Yet—it's the addition. The one and one and one seemingly ad infinitum. It's the accumulation that counts."

The phone rang, and he turned from the keyboard to answer.

It was Brian's father. A billboard had torn loose in a huge storm, knocking the car off the road. The road patrol was short-handed. They weren't found for twenty–four hours.

Dead? Yes, yes, of course. Private funerals were no longer permitted in the cities. He was arranging to bring the bodies to his small town in Central, Florida for burial.

Somehow the phone was put down. Somehow Craig found himself sobbing in Lex's arms. His Kathy. His Busy Bee. She was so golden. His sunshine. Wherever she went the world was bright. Whatever she touched she made happy and comfortable and right
. . . .

"No," Lex was saying firmly as she held him. "We cannot go get them. They are dead. We cannot—we cannot go. .

"Don't you see?" she added as the tears coursed down her own cheeks. "Don't you see, my true love? We cannot go."

He held to her a minute longer, feeling her body warm, hearing her heartbeat. Pulling a kleenex he wiped his face, pulled himself to his feet, lifting her as well.

Suddenly, fiercely he picked her up, carried her to their room, to their bed.

They held each other close until their grief turned to a frenzy of love–making; a tearing, holding, ripping of violence of love that left them exhausted and let them sleep.

INTERLUDE

China dropped the first shoe.

It was a dragon–sized shoe, and it dropped with a dragon–sized thud on the economies of the industrialized world.

Hatred of the white man had grown from a forest of shaking fists to a predatory growl; the concerted growl of the three–quarters of the planet's population that had been dismissed under the heading of the "Third World."

When China called the turn, those Third World countries, over night, repudiated the white man's debts and nationalized his indus– tries within their borders. His nationals were murdered or thrown out.

The thread that had held the Sword of Damocles over the banking world for lo these many years was snapped with the stroke of a hundred pens, proving that the pen is mightier than the sword.

It might not have made sense—but then, fear, grief, guilt and hatred seldom make sense.

The arteries of the economic world—the red blood corpuscles of money that brought oxygen to the world's cells—ruptured.

The banks, the heart of the civilization that pumped the oxygen laden red blood of cash through its body, had ceased to function.

The veins of the body of the civilization that should have carried the spent red blood cells to the lungs of commerce for cleansing, found those lungs stagnated in debt strictures, the cholesterol, that is the pneumonia of the economy.

A four–way by–pass was needed; and a clearing of the lungs so that the patient might live.

Instead its fever rose. Panic. Runs on banks for the cash that was no longer there. Industry tried to pay in script; it was not sufficient. Those who rush in to disaster to profit by buying up the bankrupt found they had no buying power.

The stock markets of the world fell like so many rocks, until they were closed by edict.

Runs on banks were stopped by governmental order that decreed bank holidays. It took longer to cut off credit–card transactions, but not much longer.

If the people had not already been in fear of the food they ate, of the water they drank, of the debts each carried, of the precariousness of their existence, solutions might have been found.

If the Para, now rampant through every nation, had not already created panic, the people might have been quieted.

Then it was learned that the President of the United States had the flu—probably Para, and that was the death knell.

The Congress could not meet—Para had deprived them of a quorum, and fear of contact with others was an unstated factor.

Stores were raided, their shelves, which never carried more than about three days' supply, were emptied. Some gas stations remained open for a while, taking I.O.Us. from known customers; but that ended when the operators were forced to supply gas at gun point. Parked cars lost their gas to siphons.

The highways emptied.

Police and soldiers alike were helpless in the face of the pandemonium, and disappeared from the streets.

In prison after prison, when the food became scarce, riots were met with riot guns, until one after another the guards succumbed and the prisoners got to the streets to wreck their own forms of havoc.

Every armed forces installation became a guarded fortress, but with short personnel since Para had decimated their ranks.

The Chief of Staff of the Pentagon declared a national curfew, and was ignored. Tanks roamed the streets, but people fled to other streets, and the tanks had to return to Base for more gas.

Individual civilian combat units were formed to guard neighborhoods, and disbanded as Para thinned their ranks.

Not even mass funerals were held now. There were few to hold them, fewer who cared to risk their own lives to attend.

People began swarming from the cities into the countryside on foot or with the last of the gasoline to power a vehicle, seeking food and water and shelter by whatever means necessary. They were met as they came, with whatever means of refusal could be found.

Orchards were stripped.

The distribution systems for food were gone with the gasoline and with a good proportion of those who normally served the system.

And always the winds and the monster hurricanes and typhoons, lashing the coasts of every nation with unbelievable force; wiping out the barrier islands; changing the coastlines.

The patient was dying.

14

There was no money.

Craig watched a growing turmoil on TV.

The great structure of banking and credit, he realized—the structure that has made possible this civilization, is being shredded.

It had nearly happened once before, back at the beginning of the Middle Ages, when the medieval Church had commanded that no usury—in practice, no interest paid on loans—could exist. That thoroughly un-real control operation had slowed—almost prevented—the development of western civilization after the fall of Rome. It was a stricture that allowed the Church to destroy the Knights Templar; that set Europe back one hundred years; that victimized the Jews—one of the reasons for its promulgation.

Its results had been nearly fatal.

Today the Third World had struck a body blow against the banks; the banks that they had importuned before in order to get the good life, though few of them had been structured for the responsibilities entailed.

Banking, they now declared, was the villain keeping them in slavery.

Well, Craig thought, banking hasn't been perfect, but since it represents the mobilization of resources, its elimination will bring on poverty, despair, ruin; not just to the Third World, but to the entire civilization, unless it can be repaired—and that over night.

Banking, and with it business and commerce, would be so disabled now as to be ineffective. They each run on trust, and that trust has been broken in a massive way. Would the condition be temporary? Permanent? There was no way to tell. Too many extraneous factors exist, he decided.

There were still news broadcasts, though not as in the old days with a cameraman in every country and the news immediate around the world.

There was still TV, but sproadic, and with very little of the former agendas. Mostly what they had been seeing recently were re-runs and commercials from stock, long since outdated.

This time there was a camera shot from out a window that showed mobs milling in the street below the station. The animal sound of a growl could be heard.

Lex was at her writing, absorbed, as though there were no world except the one of which she wrote.

There is no money, Craig thought, except that which is buried in cans and hidden in mattresses by the few.

Best, he decided, I use what we have here in the house before cash itself is declared illegal. He picked up the phone, dialed the propane company, got the manager.

"Could you top off all the tanks up here in the cove today or tomorrow?" he asked.

The voice on the other end held a frantic note. "Mr. Gallagher," it said, "you're a good customer. I'd . . . ."

He's worried I'll pay him by check or credit card, Craig decided. "I have enough cash on hand to pay you," he said. "Cash."

". . . I'd like to do anything I could," the voice was going on as though it hadn't heard, "but I have two guys out with what may be Para—and one of my drivers tried crank and went nuts. He slashed the tires of my truck .. .and ... I just don't see . . . ."

Craig looked again at the mobs still showing on TV, listened to the animal growl that rose as from one throat.

Babes in the cities, they seemed to him now. Babes whose fairy– tale `necessities' could no longer be supplied. It has been less than a hundred years, he thought, since indoor plumbing became the `right' of the civilized; less than a hundred years since electricity has lighted their homes . . . since water was delivered by the municipality . . . since they had cars and tractors and trucks to be powered by the gasoline that would now disappear; since their homes were heated by oil, now priced nearly out of reach, if it could still be had. They were like the TV figures crying "I want my Serta . . . ."

It wasn't so much that they were babes, he scolded himself. They had built their lives around the new factors as though those factors were forever.

We have failed to build an escape route from the depradations we ourselves committed.

He hung up the receiver feeling beaten, inadequate, useless.

158

I can't really believe in Yuri's two brains, he thought. I can hope he's right, that there's something different coming up—the old order changing giving place to new, lest one good custom should corrupt the world. Tennyson was quite a guy, he thought; and maybe a prophet as well.

Then he continued the quote. "Comfort thyself. What comfort is in me? . . . ."

Or I can hope that Lex is right; that a new civilization is a-birthing. But it seems far-fetched.

All I can see from where I stand is death, destruction and disaster.

We are alone, and I am afraid.

There was a roar of wind across the meadow out the window. He looked up to watch the trees bend toward the house. When he put the receiver again to his ear, it was blank. He tried to get a dial tone, but the phone was dead.

Well, he thought, it's lasted longer than I could have expected. It might be just here on the mountain, and we'll be a long time before anyone gets up here to fix it. If ever. But he knew in his bones that it wasn't just the mountain . . . or if it was, it wouldn't be for long.

As he stood watching, the TV screen turned to snow; then back to clear. A commercial of a baby hugging a roll of paper towels stuttered, went into scrambled waves . . . came back . . .and the screen went blank.

Worms, he thought. Or disolution? I'll get out the short- wave . . . find out how widespread . . . .

The lights flickered, and Lex looked up from her work.

"Damn," she said.

"You may be writing by hand for a while," he told her, and went to get the shortwave radio and its rechargeable batteries.

He inserted the batteries, held the radio, swinging it from position to position, tuned and finally got a voice. A frantic voice.

". . . it is believed the bomb fell on Chicago, although we have no confirmation yet. This is London. We have no confirmation yet . . . ."

The bomb. Man's final answer.

He went to Lex and took her in his arms, but she struggled free.

"We've got to get the others here," she was almost shouting. "Our house is the best bermed . . . the best protected. Anyhow, if we're going to be killed, we should all be together . . . ."

INTERLUDE

The first bomb dropped.

It was as though a signal had been given. The final feather had been placed.

Two more followed, but those two were extraneous.

The Earth began shaking and heaving throughout her entire body, releasing all the pent-up forces that had grown toward culmination in a violence of action that strained her to the limit.

Her waters broke across her lands; her volcanoes surged molten rock high into her atmosphere; her winds screamed across her surface; she rocked spadmodically in her orbital rotation; her crust quaked and changed.

The paroxysms climaxed in one convulsive heave.

Then she quieted.

15

The first big earthquake shook the house like a dog playing with a stick.

Craig saw his wife's face, the beginnings of terror . . . then recognition and acceptance.

"It's happening," she said, her voice loud over the turbulence.

"Get Jeff and the babies." The noise was deafening, and Craig was shouting. "I'll get Harriet and Amos. Carol and Yuri will come if they want to."

As she ran out, he grabbed the teakettle, checking to see that all the burners were out. He threw the water into the fireplace, dousing the flames.

Then he headed for the propane tank outside. A small shock . . . aftershock? . . . foreshock? . . . shook him.

He saw Lex thrown forward, catch herself on the car. She snatched the door open and was inside.

He found himself on one knee, hands in the gravel; picked himself up and staggered on to the gas tank to turn it off. Then he ran down the hill, spraddle–legged for balance, to the old log cabin, knocking loudly as he flung open the door.

Amos was bending over Harriet, his face almost gray.

"The baby's started." His voice was almost as gray as his face. "Started right after that first quake."

Craig felt his throat tighten. This, too, he thought, but his voice was calm. "We'll make a basket of our hands and carry her up," he said. "We've got to be together in the big house."

"I can walk a bit," Harriet protested, standing up. As she spoke a contraction threw her to her knees. Amos held both her hands, steadying her until it passed; then got a blanket to throw around her. Craig got water and doused the fire. Then the two men made a basket of their hands and, her arms around their necks, stag- gered out the door and up the hill, as the ground shook eradically beneath them.

The wind caught the blanket. They maneuvered it off and tossed it aside where the wind took it.

Fear was riding Craig's throat. He swallowed it, relaxing his shoulders so they could hold the girl while her stomach and legs heaved; while the ground danced; while the wind threw leaves and branches at them. He glanced at Amos who was sweating.

Unexpectedly Craig found himself remembering the time during the war when five Jap planes jumped his single fighter. Fear had threatened to tighten his muscles then, until he told himself it was an adventure; a story to tell his grandchildren. That had kept him calm. This would be one for the grandchildren too; for this coming child; and he'd tell him . . . her? the story.

Keep a smile on your face and a confident look he told himself.

When they got to the house, he led Amos, now carrying Harriet alone, through a chaos of fallen objects to the guest room, and gestured toward a chair while he stripped the bed. Then he ran to the loft, found some plastic sheeting and some old sheets Lex had stored. He fixed the bed, plastic, then a sheet, then several old sheets folded where her hips would be.

Amos was stripping the girl's clothes.

"You don't mind her naked." It was a statement, not a question.

"Better that way. We'll put a modesty sheet over her."

He looked out the window to see the two pickups parking. Lex got out carrying Dos, the other three children behind her. Jeff and Terry were emptying the pickups of plastic bags full of things they'd hastily gathered to bring.

Amos picked up Harriet and laid her on the bed, just as another contraction hit. He held her hands and she hung on, gritting her teeth against the pain.

"I think it's going to be fast," she gasped as soon as she could speak. "It feels as though it were almost here."

Craig found himself grinning. Earthquakes and babies and the wind howling outside. The end of the world is sure spectacular. Better enjoy it, he told himself. It's . . . I hope . . . a once in a lifetime experience.

Lex came in, took one startled look as she recognized the situation, then returned her husband's grin.

"Looks like we hit the jackpot," she said.

She's faced it, and she's all right. Craig was almost jubilant with relief. Win, lose or draw, they'd do their damndest—together.

Lex pulled back the 'modesty' sheet and felt the swollen abdomen. "I don't dare look inside to see whether the cervix has opened," she said. "I don't know enough. We'll just have to let nature take its course."

Unless something goes wrong, Craig thought, and found himself praying. To whom or what he didn't know, but somewhere out there . . .

The house shook again, while on the bed a contraction shook Harriet.

When the house settled and the contraction was past, Lex spoke again, her voice loud over the howling wind.

"Amos, go out and tell the others. Then do everything possible to keep them away from the windows. You're the father, but Craig and I have worked together for years."

"The kitchen doorway. It's the strongest and safest," Amos said as he left.

"Craig, go boil water, then in another pan put some twine and scissors to sterilize them. Wait! Cancel that. We can't risk fire now. Just get the scissors and string. We'll have to risk unsterilized equipment—and it's not a big risk," she added, seeing his concern. "The race survived without it for untold thousands of years."

When Craig came back, she told him briskly, "Best you sit on the bed and let Harriet hold your hands. She needs something to hold onto."

Craig took the girl's hands, and Harriet smiled. Looking into her strained face he thought, she's got guts. If we can get through this we can get through anything.

Two children from the family, he thought; two from the world at large, one on the way. Maybe Carol and Yuri would have a couple?

Seven, he decided. It's a good number. And eight adults to protect, defend, feed and keep them through whatever might come . . . an island of people in the turmoil of a world that was tearing itself apart.

He looked around. Linens had spilled from the closet; a picture on the wall had fallen; two lamps were broken on the floor; and ashtray's remains were scattered across the room—and a baby was being born.

He grinned, holding the girl's hands tightly.

Harriet's cry came as another quake shook the house. "It's coming!"

Lex flung herself onto the foot of the bed, shaking her feet loose from a blanket that had fallen to entangle them, throwing off the cover sheet.

"Push!" she demanded, holding herself as steady as possible against the shaking of the house. Craig held grimly to the girl's hands, and she put all her strength into one final effort . . . .

He heard the plop as the baby came into the world, turned to see Lex hold it to her chest, then reach for its heels.

He heard a blubbering sound, then a squall as the child started breathing. His relief came out in a sigh that seemed to come from his toes. The hands in his relaxed, and there was a smile on Harriet's face.

The house stopped shaking. Lex, still leaning against the mother's thighs, held the tiny brown body close, its umbilical cord trailing beside her, wiping its face carefully.

Then: "It's a girl," she told them, her voice raised to carry over the noise of wind and trees, lashing against the walls. "Get a towel from that pile that fell down. It will make a receiving blanket. And hand me the scissors and cord."

"Thank you," Craig whispered, again to—somewhere out there . . . .

The cord tied and cut, Lex put the baby in Craig's arms. He held it gingerly, with a warmth of love and hope. "Little bit," he whispered. "Such a little bit of preciousness . . . ."

At that moment, Harriet's body heaved again, and the huge mass of afterbirth spilled over the impromptu birthing bed—a bloody bulk of former support structure, much larger than the mass of the baby itself.

Craig leaned against the headboard, holding the tiny warmth of the baby close, watching as Lex used towels to clean the mother, gathering the discarded waste into the plastic and towels he had placed beneath the hips.

"We'll put this mess in a garbage bag." It was such a practical statement to be shouted over the noise and violence that was keeping them unsteady. Craig watched her skill with wondering eyes.

165

Then she took the baby from him and put it in Harriet's arms to nurse, holding the edge of the bed to steady herself. "It needs to nurse the minute the cord is cut," she told the girl fiercely. "I'll send Amos in and then make a place for you in the great room. We need to be together."

Meekly, Craig followed his wife out.

The sectional couch had been arranged into a square to make a playpen where the babies, Shamus and Julie would be as protected as possible. Carol and Yuri were there, and the adults had swept the mess of things, broken and unbroken, into corners. They were still working to clear the floor.

Lex went to the couch-playpen. "Can you kids make room for Harriet and the new baby when Amos brings them in?" she asked.

Shamus looked at his grandmother, his eyes pleading. "If I may get out, there'd be plenty of room," he said. "Maybe I could be some help?"

"Me too?" Julie chimed in, delighted.

"You may both get out," Lex told them. "Help if you can. If not, keep out of the way."

The house shook again, but it was a gentler shaking, a wind-in-transit shaking, as though the anger in the earth were subsiding.

Amos came in, carrying the baby, helping Harriet to the couch. She stretched out beside Uno and Dos, the newborn in one arm, the other cuddling the other two smallfry.

"Would you like to see?" she asked, pulling a corner of the towel from the tiny face.

Shamus and Julie came running to bend over the couch. Uno reached out a finger and gently touched the tiny cheek. Dos snuggled against the mother.

Lex sat down at the table. Craig found an unbroken bottle and fixed two drinks, taking them to the table. When she picked hers up, her hand was shaking, and it spilled.

"As though there weren't enough mess." Craig could hardly hear her. Her eyes were wet.

He leaned over with a dishrag and wiped up the spill, then put his hand over hers.

"We're all going to stay here until we're sure what's happening," he told her. "It may be crowded . . . ."

"Of course," she said.

"It may be quite a while?" Terry's voice was shy. "We . . . ."

"We need to be together." Lex smiled feebly. Craig saw that she was smothering the shakes that were trying to take over her whole body. He wanted to take her in his arms, to tell her he was proud of her, but held himself back. He knew instinctively that this was not the time.

Abruptly she put her head on the table, sobbing.

"It doesn't matter," he could hear her saying through her sobs. "It doesn't matter. The baby's born and she's safe. You're here and you're safe. We're all together and that's the only thing that matters."

On the other side of the room, Shamus was standing beside Amos as the big man folded clothes into a pile.

"Weren't you scared when the baby came?" Shamus asked. "Grandma was. You can tell. Her hands were shaking."

Craig listened intently for the answer. It would be important. Amos was looking down at the tow–head, then he sat on his heels beside the boy.

"Of course I was scared," he told the youngster. "We're all scared. Be idiots if we weren't. But I'm not half as scared now as I have been out there in a world where there was little understanding and less love."

Then Amos stood up, his huge form dominating the room. His face broke into a big grin, and he spoke loudly. "When you're scared," he said, "it's time to get busy. We're together. We can face anything the Good Lord cares to send along."

Craig looked around, watching face after face light up. He felt his own courage coming back; felt unjustified hope creep through his body.

It was as though they had found themselves to be an independent whole, here on their mountain, with the shards of their former civilization around them; a unit that could grow, keeping the heritage of the past, building a new future.

It's not the end, he thought. It's the beginning. Like a covered wagon setting off into a strange world with only what they could carry to build with.

The shaking had stopped completely now. Even the storm had ceased its fury.

167

He looked around. Harriet and the babies were in the play-pen couch. Shamus and Julie were making themselves busy. Terry, Jeff, Amos, Yuri and Carol had each taken up a task. Lex was still at the table, pulling herself together. The quiet was intense.

Then he felt it: a quivering in the floor. A quivering as of a light drum far in the distance; a beating he could only feel through the soles of his feet.

"Lie down!" he shouted. "Everybody lie on the floor. Quick!"

He grabbed Julie to his side, lying down with her under his shoulder.

The quivering grew until it was a drumbeat inside his skull, a churning throughout his body and the smaller body he held close.

That was when the big quake hit. A monster quake; a ferocious roaring quake that threw them from side to side across the floor. A battering nightmare of an earthquake, accompanied by sheets of rain and wind more violent than anything yet, and of cannons of explosive sound.

A big tree at the corner of the house crashed across the deck, its branches catching on a corner of the roof and on the railing of the deck, making a cave around the windows. At the far end of the house there was another crash, and he knew that a tree had hit the house there.

Craig held Julie to him, forcing his head up to see who had been hurt; counting noses; listening for voices.

The storm outside, he realized wonderingly, was silenced as though cut off by some giant hand. The wind had ceased. The rain no longer lashed at the walls. The house was still.

The silence was a palpable thing.

Then Uno, Dos and the new baby squalled, precipitately and lustily; and Craig found he could breathe again.

Slowly he crawled across the floor, Julie in his arms, reaching to each of them, to touch them, to be reassured.

Then he lay back, breathing deeply, quietly.

The earth shuddered once more with an almost passive relaxation.

It would be the last, he knew; not consciously but with a deep atavistic knowledge, as though from some ancient well of comprehension, long buried.

He lay quiet, resting, feeling familiarity deep in his flesh.

They were alone. Alone in a world he would hardly recognize. A world in which they were isolated beyond belief.

Yet they were a unit . . . and the crisis was past.

He turned his eyes to the gable window. The clouds were heavy, but somehow comforting. The sun would break through after a time. The earth beneath would warm into spring.

It would be a young world again; a world renewed.

POSTLUDE

It was over.

The long gestation, nearly six thousand years, was ended. The Earth lay trembling quietly after the vast tumult. Her internal melt was slowly ebbing into calm. Her crust no longer heaved with the ferocity of the birthing.

Heavy clouds obscured her from the sun, but these would dissipate. Darkness was necessary to the little ones.

The great bulk of the scurrying beings that had eaten her substance to nourish the true fetus—the afterbirth of her confinement— was decaying into her soil, a compost that would give it back much of its lost nourishment.

The newborns were scattered across her surface, like a litter of pups, and would soon be ready to nurse at her widely separated teats.

Presently she would nourish the weak beings, but for now she simply lay quiescent.

The birthing was over. The new life could grow slowly to an independent maturity, under her care.

Her body could return to the slow pulsing, the abundance, the vitality it would need in the warding of her children.

The kids were urging their horses up the mountain, waving and shouting. He caught the word "Minstrel."

The Wandering Minstrel of the Mountains would be coming. The horseback crew would carry the message, and everyone left within reach would gather, for there would be news and singing and a hoe–down. The Minstrel could fiddle up a mean dance tune.

Craig stretched his lean, hard body, taking pleasure in its mus– cular condition.

It had been a rough ten years, but rewarding.

The first year had been the marauding vandals, with the food– stocks dwindling.

The second was worse. The vandals were almost extinct by then, but food! The books had helped. Books on edible plants, on soap– making, on gardening and preserving the seeds for the next year. They still had not dared go as far as the river to fish.

Slowly, slowly they'd learned. They'd hardened. They'd grown together. They'd survived.

He looked through the clean air to the darkening sky, to the first stars beginning to appear, brilliant again now that the smog no longer hid them. By full dark they'd be sparkling from horizon to horizon.

Thank you, he whispered. To someone. To somewhere. Out there.